"The Better Angels of Our Nature":
What if the American Civil War didn't happen?
by
Bob Faser

Brimstone Books: Hobart

Copyright © 2017, Robert J. Faser

Published by Brimstone Books, Hobart, Tasmania, Australia

All rights reserved.

ISBN-10: 1977884962

ISBN-13: 978-1977884961

A Note to the Reader

This book is a work of fiction. It does not pretend to be otherwise. In fact, this book is my first attempt at writing book-length fiction.

This book is part of the style of historical fiction called an "historical counterfactual" or an "alternate history". It does not pretend to be accurate history. If you want to learn more about this particular style of historical fiction, please read the section "Why I wrote this book" at the end of the book. Depending on your preferences, you can read this section either before you read the main part of the book, or afterwards, or even both if you so choose.

Most of the people in this narrative are actual, historical people, even if they are placed in fictional, counterfactual situations. Others are fictitious creations. I have identified fictitious characters in this narrative by placing their names *in italics*. For example, the character *Figaro Johnson* (mentioned above) is fictitious. On a number of occasions, I have placed characters from fiction (some American, some British) into my narrative. Their names are also *in italics*.

I hope you enjoy reading this book. I enjoyed writing it. If you *do* enjoy this book, please make sure you write a review for this book on the ***Amazon*** or ***CreateSpace*** website, depending on which site you bought this book from. Another thing you can do if you enjoy the book is to buy multiple copies as gifts for friends or family members.

Remember, books make great gifts! (They're also very easy to gift-wrap.)

>Bob Faser
>Hobart, Tasmania, Australia
>3rd October 2017

1. "Gentlemen, what do the better angels of *your* nature say to you"?

Washington, April 11 1861:

"The news from Charleston is dire," Abraham Lincoln told his cabinet. The recently-inaugurated President appeared to have aged twenty years in the past month.

"General Beauregard is determined to take Fort Sumter. Major Anderson and his men inside the fort are running out of food and ammunition. The Confederates will not let the relief fleet into the harbour. Do we relieve Sumter and make an armed rebellion inevitable? Do we withdraw from Sumter, and allow our Union to disintegrate? What do you think, gentlemen?"

A stony silence fell across the room.

After a few seconds, which seemed like an hour, the President continued "As for me, I cannot allow this tension between our states to erupt into bloodshed. When I was inaugurated, I spoke of our duty to follow 'the better angels of our nature'. ... As for me, the better angels of *my* nature cannot accept the idea of young men from Maine and young men from Louisiana training to kill each other. ... The better angels of *my* nature cannot accept the idea of Pennsylvania soldiers marching through Georgia as a hostile army. ... The better angels of *my* nature cannot accept the idea of Texan and Wisconsin regiments firing on each other. ... The better angels of *my* nature cannot accept the shots fired by a good young man from Mississippi causing tears to flow in a Connecticut cemetery. ... The better angels of *my* nature cannot accept the idea of families from Virginia, or Maryland, or Tennessee, or my native Kentucky torn apart with brothers fighting on opposite sides."

"Sadly, I will have failed either to save the Union or to remove the stain of slavery from this land, but I cannot order these good young men to kill other good young men in the name of either worthy cause. I pray that some later President will end the evil of slavery, and that some later President will restore this Union. Those later Presidents, however, will not be me."

"Gentlemen, I propose that we send orders to Major Anderson to accept General Beauregard's terms. I further propose that Mr. Seward and I will seek to meet with Mr. Davis at the earliest possible opportunity. I finally propose that we send some of our most senior statesmen, regardless of their party, to meet with the governors and other officials of those Southern states that have not yet seceded. Perhaps we can delay their decision and save at least some of the Union."

"Gentlemen," the President concluded, "what do the better angels of *your* nature say to you"?

2. Negotiating a settlement

Washington, April 16 1861

On the Tuesday morning following the surrender of Fort Sumter, six men, five civilian politicians and a military officer, met in the President's office.

The President began. "Time is of the essence, Gentlemen. Three of us will meet with the Confederate leaders within the next few weeks: Secretary Seward, Colonel Lee and myself. I've received a telegram from Mr. Davis agreeing in principle to a meeting. We still need to organise a location and a date. During the time I'm involved in the negotiations, I'll ask you, Mr. Vice-President, to serve as Acting President." Hannibal Hamlin nodded in agreement.

"While we're organising this, there is one urgent task. Senator Douglas and Senator Johnson, your task will be to visit the governors and other senior politicians of each of the eight slave states that have not seceded. I hope that cooler heads may prevail in each of these states and that they will not follow the seven states which have seceded."

"Will Steve and I be travelling together, or separately?" asked the Senator from Tennessee.

"Together, I'd hope," replied the President. "Having a pair from the North and the South together communicates our desire to keep the southern states (or, at least, as many southern states as possible) as equal partners in our Union."

"Bill, who do you think will be the members of the Confederate negotiating group?" the Colonel asked the Secretary of State.

"Well, Bob," replied the Secretary of State. "Jeff Davis has indicated his fellow-negotiators will be the Secretary of State and the Attorney-General."

Colonel Lee replied, "Toombs is a fool, even when he's sober, which isn't often. On the other hand, Judah Benjamin has one of the best minds in the land."

William Seward added, "My idea is that our strategy should emphasise flattery towards Davis and Toombs, while assuming that Benjamin will be the serious negotiator for the Confederates." Lincoln nodded sagely.

Stephen Douglas looked at the rapidly aged Lincoln at his desk and gave a silent prayer of thanks that he lost the previous year's election. "When do Andy and I leave?"

"As soon as possible, Steve," said Seward. "Begin with Delaware, and work westwards. It may take all summer."

3. A House Divided

The politicians and statesmen began their work.

Stephen Douglas and Andrew Johnson began their journey of many months from Dover in late April to Jefferson City in early September. With the secession of the seven Confederate states being treated by the United States as a *fait accompli*, there seemed little urgency among the leaders of the border states to join them, particularly with the question of abolition being taken off the table.

- In Delaware, secession was never really considered an option.
- In Arkansas, the economy was too closely linked to the port of New Orleans for the state not to secede after Louisiana seceded.
- Otherwise, the border states took a "wait-and-see" attitude and chose not to secede for the time being.

There were two main results of the Douglas-Johnson mission:

- The Confederate secession was limited to eight states, the seven states that had seceded prior to Fort Sumter plus Arkansas.
- The two senators had developed a close working relationship with each other, a working relationship with ramifications on later political events.

While they were in Richmond, meeting with the governor and legislators of Virginia, Douglas read a newspaper report of a typhoid outbreak in Chicago. He wrote to his wife encouraging her and their children to leave the city urgently for the sake of their health.

Meanwhile, negotiations between the senior figures of the United States and the Confederacy began in early May, in Raleigh. It was seen as a good symbol that the talks would be held in a state whose legislature had not yet made up its mind regarding secession.

Lee and Seward were right about the dynamic among the Confederate negotiators. Secretary of State Robert Toombs was rarely sober enough to contribute anything more than the occasional coarse remark or ribald joke to the discussions. Jefferson Davis was often vague and frequently distracted by trivial aspects of the discussions. Attorney General Judah Benjamin became, by default, the main serious negotiator for the Confederacy.

The three Union negotiators functioned as more of a coherent team. The suave, urbane, well-travelled Seward and the practical, folksy, man-of-the-people Lincoln provided a contrast in emphases, with Lee making his particular contributions when the perspective of a Southerner, or that of a military man, was needed.

At the end of the negotiations, which lasted for two months, a number of principles were established:

- The secession of the eight Confederate states, along with the future secession of any other states, was accepted (*de facto* if not *de jure*) by the Union.

- The Union declared that any state which had seceded will be welcomed back into the United States whenever the state government applied for re-admission.

- While the continuation or the abolition of slavery was seen as a matter for individual states, both sides affirmed privately that the era of slavery in North America was coming to an end.

- There was to be a free movement of people and goods between the Union and the Confederacy. (The extent to which this applied to slaves was deliberately vague.)

- The Indian Territory (between Texas and Kansas) and the New Mexico Territory (between Texas and California) were proclaimed as the Protectorates, essentially self-governing homelands for Native American tribes under the joint jurisdiction of the Union and the Confederacy, as well as serving as a buffer region between Texas, California, and the Mormon settlements in the Utah Territory.

These principles, when they were written in their final agreed form, were signed by Lincoln, Seward, and Lee for the Union; and by Davis, Toombs, and Benjamin for the Confederacy. In the Confederacy, they were called the Treaty of Raleigh while, in the Union (still reluctant to view the Confederacy as a foreign nation and, as a result, also reluctant to use the language of a "treaty"), they were called the Principles of Raleigh. Nevertheless, they provided the beginning of a framework for a peaceful relationship between the Union and the Confederacy for the sixty-five years of their separate existence.

4. "... the delicate morality of a Massachusetts schoolmaster or a Quaker spinster ..."

One person with a particular interest in the Principles of Raleigh first read them in the **Deseret News** while sitting in his study in Salt Lake City. Brigham Young, President and Prophet of the Church of Jesus Christ of Latter-Day Saints saw the Union's acceptance of the secession of the Confederate states to be a golden opportunity for his Mormon followers to establish their own independence.

Through the LDS church, he called for a territorial convention in the Utah Territory to discuss secession from the United States. The convention eventually met – without the approval of the territorial governor - in Salt Lake City in March of 1862. While those attending were overwhelmingly Latter-Day Saints, they were seen as a legitimate representation of the population of the territory. 60% of the convention voted to secede from the United States and establish the Commonwealth of Deseret.

The secession conference in Salt Lake City said nothing about slavery in the future Commonwealth of Deseret, or about whether Deseret would join the Confederacy or go it alone. These decisions were left in the hands of any future government for the Commonwealth.

This decision provided the first test of the cordial relations between Washington and Montgomery.

On the one hand, no one in the Confederate leadership wanted Deseret in the Confederacy. Davis knew that a polygamous Deseret would be a divisive influence in the

Confederacy. On the other hand, the Confederacy saw a possible recognition of Deseret by Washington as an increased affirmation of the Confederacy's legitimacy. In any event, the Confederacy was reluctant for its act of secession to be associated with Deseret and its practice of polygamy.

As far as the Union was concerned, it was happy to be rid of the issue of polygamy in the Utah Territory, but it was reluctant to lose any further territory.

Then there was the question of slavery in Deseret. Some of the settlers, Mormon and otherwise, in the Utah Territory (particularly those who were from the southern states themselves) held slaves. Young himself was pro-slavery. Still, the vast majority of Mormons were strongly anti-slavery, as was the founder of the LDS Church, the late Joseph Smith.

The possible mixture of slavery and polygamy in the same jurisdiction was a potentially explosive situation that threatened to undermine the whole agreement reached at Raleigh. The telegraph lines between Washington and Montgomery ran hot.

Finally, Jefferson Davis addressed this issue in a speech to the joint houses of the Confederate Congress.

"Gentlemen, we need to be clear and firm regarding the developments in the Utah Territory. There is no room in the Confederacy for the practice of polygamy. While we recognise the right of the people of Deseret to secede from the United States, as each of our own states has done, we will not welcome into the Confederacy any state in which polygamy is an accepted practice. (*applause*) ... As well, we need to be careful with any of our slaves who may be brought to Deseret or sold to citizens of Deseret. Call me old-fashioned, but I believe slaveholders have a moral responsibility for those who labour on our behalf. (*applause*) ... Many of our slaves, both male and female, have the delicate morality of a Massachusetts schoolmaster (*laughter*) or a Quaker spinster (*more laughter*) and we cannot allow them to be morally corrupted by the sight of masters with large harems of multiple wives and concubines. (*wild applause and cheering*) ...."

Following Davis's oration, both houses of the Confederate Congress unanimously passed two resolutions:

1. Resolved, the Confederate States of America will never admit the Commonwealth of Deseret (or any other applicant for statehood) as a state for such time as the practice of polygamy is legal in such jurisdiction.

2. Resolved, the Confederate States of America regards it as a criminal offense for any of its citizens to transport any slave to any jurisdiction permitting polygamy, or to sell any slave to a resident of any jurisdiction permitting polygamy.

In his memoirs, written while in exile in Montreal, Davis wrote, "Of course, I admit that, in my speech, I consciously exploited the widespread hypocrisy regarding race and sex that was (and is) common both north and south of the border. Looking at my colleagues sitting before me, I knew many men with good and legitimate reasons to believe that their valet was also their half-brother, or even their son. And yes, of course, my comments about 'the delicate morality of a Massachusetts schoolmaster or a Quaker spinster' catered to our own Southern image of Yankee prissiness. I do not apologise for this to one iota. The Confederate States, in their infancy, could not tolerate the existence of polygamy within their life. We would fragment and shatter. I did what I could to prevent the disruptive presence of Deseret within our Confederate community."

In a similar vein, Willian Seward wrote to a friend "In many ways, while I deplore his embrace of slavery as a way of life, this one speech was the single master-stroke of Jeff Davis's political life."

Within a few weeks of the resolutions of the Confederate Congress, a similar resolution banning any slaveholder within the Union from transporting or selling any slave to Deseret or any other jurisdiction allowing polygamy also overwhelmingly passed both houses of the United States Congress.

Those speaking eloquently in favour of these motions included a mixture of slaveholders and ardent abolitionists. There were a number of humourous allusions to Davis's references to "Massachusetts schoolmasters" and "Quaker spinsters".

On the 24th of July 1862, the 15th anniversary of the arrival of the first Mormon pioneers in the Salt Lake Valley, the General Assembly of the Commonwealth of Deseret proclaimed the Commonwealth to be a sovereign nation, independent of both the United States of America and of the Confederate States of America. As well, slavery was to be forever abolished from the Commonwealth of Deseret. Finally, the Commonwealth of Deseret declared its desire to sign the Raleigh agreement, a desire to which the governments in both Washington and Montgomery reluctantly agreed. As Robert Toombs crudely observed (in a rare moment of sobriety) to his colleagues in the Confederate cabinet, "It's better to have Deseret inside the tent pissing out, than to have them outside the tent, pissing in."

5. The beginning of the end for slavery

In many ways, Deseret was one of the least of Jefferson Davis's problems.

The Confederacy depended on the export of cotton for its economy to thrive. The cotton-producing states all seceded, while the non-cotton-producing states chose to remain in the Union, at least for the time being. The economy of the Confederacy depended on cotton being sent to Europe.

However, the cotton warehouses of Britain and France were full. Cloth producers, fearing a war, bought large quantities of cotton in the event that the supply of cotton would be cut off. European cotton buyers were offering insultingly low prices for Confederate cotton.

To make matters worse, other cotton-growing countries, including India and Egypt, increased their production in anticipation of a shortage of American cotton. In some of Britain's Australian colonies, cotton production was beginning. Of course, the owners of British mills would be under particular pressure to buy Indian or Australian cotton, to keep the profits within the Empire. Mills in the New England states still wanted southern cotton, but the Yankee demand for cotton was far less than the quantity of cotton the Confederacy was growing. Within a few years, "King Cotton" would be forced off his economic throne in the Confederacy.

However, the Confederacy's economic woes were not yet obvious to many people north of the border. Lincoln,

Davis, and their Secretaries of State spent much of August of 1862 negotiating on the possibilities of an exchange of diplomats between Washington and Montgomery.

Both diplomats were already well-known by senior officials in each other's capitals, having been involved in the Raleigh negotiations. Colonel Robert E. Lee was appointed as the United States' Minister to the Confederacy, while Attorney-General Judah P. Benjamin became the Confederacy's envoy to Washington. Both appointments were hailed as brilliant by the press on both sides of the border.

When it came to selecting envoys to Salt Lake City, the choices were somewhat less well heralded, yet well-received.

The Union's Minister to the Commonwealth of Deseret was the Irish-born Thomas Francis Meagher, a former Irish rebel and prisoner of the British in the Van Diemen's Land penal colony in Australia. On escaping his imprisonment, he made his way to New York where he edited a newspaper for the Irish-American community of the city.

The Confederacy's man in Salt Lake City was Colonel Edmund Kirby Smith, a Floridian and a former mathematics instructor at West Point. Kirby Smith arrived in Salt Lake City accompanied by his recent bride Cassie and by his valet, a mixed-race slave named Alexander Darnes, who bore an uncanny resemblance to Kirby Smith. Rumours that Kirby Smith and Darnes were half-brothers persisted throughout both men's lives, into Kirby Smith's career as a diplomat, mathematics professor, and political leader, and into Darnes's medical practice in Jacksonville.

Other than the appointment of diplomats, throughout 1863, the thoughts of Washington's political powerbrokers began to turn to the 1864 election.

General John C Fremont, the Republican candidate in 1856, was emerging as the candidate for those who wanted to take military action against the eight Confederate states and force them back into the Union. Massachusetts Senator Charles Sumner, once beaten nearly to death on the floor of the Senate for his strong support of Abolition, was regarded to be his likeliest running-mate.

Senators Stephen Douglas of Illinois and Andrew Johnson of Tennessee were emerging as the ticket for those wishing to woo the Confederate States back into the Union by granting almost any concession they requested. Douglas was the Democrats' 1860 candidate, and he and Johnson were well-regarded for their efforts in keeping seven of the fifteen slave states within the Union.

In all this, "Will Abe run again?" was the question. If not, who would be the candidate defending the Lincoln legacy against the Fremont-Sumner and Douglas-Johnson tickets: Hamlin?, … Seward?, … Lee?, … anyone else?

But, the most important news of 1863 didn't take place in Washington, or Montgomery, or Salt Lake City. **The North Carolina Standard**, published in Raleigh and edited by William Woods Holden, one of the most vocal opponents of secession in the southern states, published a signed editorial by Holden with the title "An end to slavery and a renewed prosperity" in February of 1863. The editorial declared that the continuation of slavery would lead the southern states (both those which seceded and those – such as North Carolina – which didn't) to continued economic stagnation.

A process of gradual and voluntary – or (more accurately) semi-voluntary – emancipation in which slaveholders were compensated for the loss of their slaves, and in which freed slaves were given funds to start themselves off in farms or in other occupations, would be the source of a dynamic, new economic vitality for the South.

Holden's editorial was hotly debated around the Southern states for most of 1863.

South of the border, in the cotton states which seceded, the article was dismissed, even if the cotton slump was beginning to cause economic pain.

In the slaveholding states which didn't secede, which were far less dependent on labour-intensive cotton-growing, Holden's argument made far more sense. In May, the North Carolina legislature passed a law which became the model for semi-voluntary emancipation schemes in other states:

- A person born to a parent who was a slave was free from the moment of birth.
- Slaves could no longer be sold.

- Every slave was assigned a state-determined cash value, reviewed annually, depending on the slave's age, health, gender, and skills.

- If a slave (or a person acting in the interest of the slave) could pay the cash value to the slaveholder, the slaveholder was legally required to free the slave.

- At the death of a slaveholder, the slaves are either freed, or retained by the slaveholder's heir upon the payment of a tax of 150% of the slave's cash value (which was paid into the state's Manumission Fund).

- If a slaveholder voluntarily frees a slave, the slaveholder was paid 200% of the slave's cash value by the Manumission Fund. The slave was paid a similar amount by the Fund as start-up money to establish themselves independently.

- The Manumission Fund was financed (in addition to the inheritance taxes on slaves) by the selling of Manumission Bonds, interest-bearing securities sold to individuals and companies by the State Government.

The scheme was a money-maker for all concerned. Many people (particularly northern Abolitionists and "free people of colour") bought large quantities of Manumission Bonds. Slaveholders freed their slaves and used the money to upgrade their properties. Former slaves had money to establish themselves as independently free people. Cash was circulating around the state. Within a year, all the other slaveholding states within the Union had established similar schemes. South of the border, the scheme was even debated in a few state legislatures in response to the growing cotton crisis.

An interesting side-factor was that very few Manumission Bonds were ever cashed in in to the relevant government departments. Holders of bonds – particularly those of Abolitionist leanings - put their Bonds into frames and hung them on their walls as if they were works of art. By the turn of the century, a genuine Manumission Bond could be sold to an antiques dealer for three times its face value. North Carolina Bonds, being the earliest, would be sold for five times the face value, depending on the date. Delaware Bonds, being the rarest, would have attracted an even higher price.

Prices on Manumission Bonds have continued to increase. Today, even a comparatively common Tennessee or Virginia Manumission Bond (or a much more common post-coup Confederate States Manumission Bond) in reasonable condition would attract a price at open auction comparable to that of a Joe DiMaggio rookie card in mint condition. Deseret "Monogamy Bonds" from the 1880s and 1890s, along with jointly-issued Union-Confederate-Deseret Manumission Bonds from the time of the Great War, are also particularly popular among collectors.

6. "This here boy is my slave, and I'm a-fixin' to set him free. Where do we get our money?"

In the town of Beckley, Virginia, late on a Friday afternoon in late August of 1865, two young men, one white and one black, walked into Raleigh County Court House to see the county clerk. The clerk was about to shut up his office for the weekend.

With a broad hillbilly-like accent, the white man pointed to the black man and said to the clerk, "This here boy is my slave, and I'm a-fixin' to set him free. Where do we get our money?"

The black man grunted inarticulately and said "Yessir," like a field hand.

The clerk looked for the forms and the cash box in his desk, while the pair stiffened.

They've done this before.

The two young men were from small towns in Maryland. They met while they were apprentice tailors in Baltimore. During this time, they always talked about opening their own tailor shop, specialising in fine, English-style, made-to-measure men's suits. They had the skills. All they needed was the money to start out.

Elijah Murphy, the black man, was from a family of "free persons of colour" on the Eastern Shore. "We were free since before the War of 1812," he often boasted. "We took our family name not from some slaveowners, but from the gentle and kind Irish midwife who delivered my grandfather's oldest brother, the first freeborn *Murphy*."

George MacKenzie, the white man, was from western Maryland. "We were Quakers," he often said, "who were strongly against the idea that people should own other people as slaves".

When their apprenticeships were completed, about the time that the first Manumission Law was passed in North Carolina, they hit on a plan. They'd get the money for their business with some of that manumission money that was going around.

They had to prepare themselves. Both had a good standard of schooling, cultured accents, enlightened attitudes, and high standards of personal hygiene. They had to make themselves sound and look like a hillbilly and a field hand, neither of whom could read or write. *MacKenzie* had to learn how to use words like "boy" and "nigger" casually and convincingly when referring to *Murphy*, while *Murphy* had to learn the slave's art of acting subserviently to his "massa". They both also had to achieve that exact level of ripe B.O. to have the effect of adding to their sense of authenticity, while also increasing the urgency of the clerk's desire to give them the money quickly and get them out of his office.

They also developed a bit of patter about their future plans, carefully avoiding any mention of either tailoring or Baltimore. *Murphy* had a modest story about "chicken farmin' out west in Missouri" with his uncle. *Mackenzie* spun an ambitious story about "goin' up north to Maine, buyin' me a boat, and doin' some of that lobster fishin'," adding "I hear there's good money in them lobsters."

They arrived in a county seat and started researching the local scene. ... Where were the remote outposts in the county where a person could claim to be from when showing up in town and still be believed even if no one recognised him, usually places with names such as Snake Belly Hollow? ... At what time of the week was the county clerk most likely to be in a hurry to shut up the office and go home? ... At what time of the month was the county clerk under pressure to show his reports to the state officials and say, "Yes, I've been actively providing the Manumission Fund money to applicants"? ... What are the differences between the local accent and the local slang to the accent and slang of the last place they were?

They've done this all before, twenty-four times over the past two years to be exact, in rural county seats across North Carolina, Virginia, Kentucky, and Tennessee. (Maryland and Delaware were too close to home. The pair didn't need to travel as far west as Missouri.) They lived on some of the money, while saving most. After today, they should have the money they need. *Mr. Solomon*, the Baltimore tailor to whom they were once apprenticed, was retiring. He wanted to sell his business by the end of the year, but he'd rather sell the business to his former apprentices than to a stranger. After today's efforts, the pair should have enough saved to buy the business, premises, and stock, to buy a pair of modest houses, and to marry their fiancees (after buying the freedom of *Murphy*'s fiancée, a cook in the home of an elderly, wealthy widow in Annapolis.)

While they were on their way out of town to take some hot baths and burn their smelly "swindling clothes", *Elijah Murphy* said, "Well, *George*, it's time for us to stop swindling and start tailoring."

(Note: In 1950, the Baltimore menswear store Mackenzie and Murphy's, whose advertising slogan "London quality at Maryland prices" was a perpetual source of material for local humourists, was sold to a national department store chain. The decision to sell was made by the Mackenzie and Murphy families when no member of the younger generation of either family wanted to go into the business, preferring legal, medical, or academic careers. The department store chain kept the Mackenzie and Murphy's name for their premium menswear lines. During its time in business, Mackenzie and Murphy's was known for their generous donations to of a large number of medical, educational, and charitable causes, both locally and nationally. While rumours persisted about the dodgy means by which the business raised its initial capital, the amount paid in donations over eighty-five years of business was at least twenty times the most generous estimate of what George and Elijah would have received for their swindles in the 1860s.)

7. "Are you with us, Jim?"

Montgomery, April 1864

> *Oh, we ain't got food and we can't eat cotton.*
> *Something in Montgomery's rotten.*
> *Look away, look away, look away, Dixie Land!*

As Major-General James Longstreet walked down the street to General Beauregard's house, he heard a drunken man singing these words to the tune of a popular minstrel song. The song, *Dixie*, had been regarded as the Confederacy's unofficial anthem in the years since 1861, and General Longstreet was disheartened to hear it parodied to express such hopelessness and despair. But then, at least he wasn't singing about a desire to "hang Jeff Davis from a sour apple tree", as he heard a group of equally drunk Louisiana infantrymen singing, in the words of a pre-Sumter Yankee marching song, one night last week.

He arrived at his commander's home and handed his hat to the butler at the door. He was shown into the General's office.

"Thank you for coming so quickly, Jim," said the General. "The situation is worsening. The riots in New Orleans are beginning to spread to other cities: … Charleston, … Savannah, … Columbia … Atlanta …. People are hungry. Food is becoming too expensive. We can't produce enough food because our prime agricultural land is covered in cotton plants. We can buy plenty of food from the north but, by the time it gets here, the price of bringing it down makes it too expensive for working people to buy. And the politicians are dithering. It's time for the Army to act, Jim. Are you with us?"

8. Abraham Lincoln and his legacy

Washington, April 1864

At the same time as two generals in Montgomery were discussing a possible coup, three politicians and a diplomat gathered in Washington to discuss a more peaceful transfer of political power.

Abraham Lincoln looked at the three men sitting with him in his office: Hannibal Hamlin, his loyal if somewhat colourless Vice-President; ... William Seward, his suave and worldly Secretary of State; ... and Robert E. Lee, the patrician army officer turned diplomat. He wanted these men, his inner circle, to be the first (other than members of his family) to hear his decision.

"Gentlemen, we have an election later this year. Every President since Martin Van Buren has been content with serving a single term in office. I do not wish to change this tradition. I've promised Mary and the boys that I'll stand aside for another President. We're planning to travel. London beckons. Paris beckons. Rome, Jerusalem, even India and Australia, all beckon. I owe it to Mary. I believe that my successor – and possibly even my successor's successor – is sitting in this room. Whichever one of the three of you will be that president, you will have my full support, even if it will be from a distance."

In saying these words, Lincoln looked and sounded much older that his fifty-five years.

Seward stood up and, after expressing gratitude to Lincoln for his leadership, continued, "I, for one, am not a candidate either. I once had ambitions for this office, but I hold these ambitions no longer." Looking at Hamlin and Lee, he said, "Whichever one of you becomes President, sir, you will have my support as well as Mr. Lincoln's, and, as well, if you wish me to continue in this role of Secretary of State, I will serve your administration with the same energy I gave to the present one."

Hamlin and Lee looked at each other. Neither wanted the job. Hamlin was content in his role as Vice-President. Lee enjoyed the job of maintaining good relations between the Union and Confederate governments. Both saw how the pressures of the job had affected Abe. However, both were concerned about the alternatives to either of them.

Radical Republicans were encouraging a Fremont-Sumner ticket, with the intent of forcing the Confederacy (and, depending on to whom you spoke, Deseret as well) back into the Union by force.

Democrats from slave states were encouraging a Douglas-Johnson ticket with the intent of making sufficient concessions to slaveholders to make rejoining the Union an attractive prospect to the Confederacy, even if the New England states were similarly tempted to secede in the process.

It fell to Robert E. Lee to break the silence. "Gentlemen, I believe that President Lincoln's legacy needs to be preserved. A Fremont-Sumner or Douglas-Johnson administration would fragment our fragile Republic to an even greater extent than it has suffered in the past few years. A ticket led by Mr. Hamlin from a New England state, supported by myself, from a Southern state, would have the widest appeal, particularly if we can guarantee Mr. Seward's ongoing leadership in the State Department. If Mr. Hamlin would consent to serve as President, I would be honoured to serve as his Vice-President and, if necessary, his successor."

Lincoln and Seward smiled.

Hannibal Hamlin solemnly accepted his fate.

9. A Bloodless Coup

Montgomery, May 1864

Beauregard and Longstreet entered the Confederate Capitol building. A regiment of soldiers surrounded the building.

The two generals were nervous. *Coups-d'etat* were not in their line of work.

The building seemed eerily empty as they entered. Were they walking into a trap?

An elderly porter was the first person they saw. "Good morning, Generals," he said. "There aren't too many people around here today. Mister Davis and the cabinet heard yesterday you all were a-coming today with some soldiers and they all just skedaddled. Mister Benjamin seems to be in charge and he's in Mister Davis's office waiting for you all."

"What is he doing?" asked Beauregard.

"Well, the last time I looked, he seemed to be smoking one of Mr. Davis's cigars and drinking some of his good French brandy. He's in a good mood, too. He gave me a bottle to take home, as well as a box of good cigars."

The officers proceeded to the President's office and saw that it was all as the old man had described. The Confederacy's chief diplomat in Washington was sitting at the President's desk drinking French cognac and smoking a Cuban cigar.

"Welcome, gentlemen," said Judah Benjamin. "Pull up a chair. Grab a glass and a cigar. I gather Roscoe told you I'm the only civilian official in the building. I actually suspect I'm the only civilian official left in all Montgomery. I only turned up yesterday to deliver my quarterly report to the cabinet and found there was no one around to report to, as they were all on their way out of town."

"Where are they all?" asked Longstreet.

"Well, Jim, as far as Jeff Davis is concerned, he's on a train heading in the direction of Montréal, accompanied by his pregnant wife and his young daughter. I imagine he's been out of Confederate territory since sometime last night. Toombs is probably sleeping off a hangover somewhere. The others have all left town and gone to their homes."

Pointing to a stack of papers on the desk, he said, "The letters of resignation are all there, including mine. As the senior remaining civilian official of the government of the Confederate States of America, I hereby transfer all political power in the Confederacy to you two gentlemen. Good luck, Jim. *Bonne chance*, Pierre. You'll need it."

10. Executive Order Number 28

Away from Montgomery, the Confederate coup remained as bloodless as it was in Montgomery. State governments, except for Texas, voluntarily ceded their powers to the Provisional Administration, led by a Committee of Public Safety

The Committee, made up of the two generals plus Judah Benjamin (who was persuaded by Beauregard and Longstreet – along with a few more glasses of Jefferson Davis's excellent cognac - to join the Committee), purchased large amounts of grain cheaply from the Union and from Canada, a course of action the previous government was unwilling to take. With more food available, and the food riots ceasing, the junta was able to focus on more long-range issues.

The main issue was the amount of arable land used in producing cotton, rather than food. The greater the amount of land that produced food to be eaten locally, rather than cotton to be sent to mills in Europe, the better it would be for the Confederacy's economic and social well-being. This meant that agriculture in the Confederacy needed to shift from large plantations worked by slaves to small, family farms, worked by free people.

In July of 1864, the Committee on Public Safety of the Provisional Administration of the Confederate States of America, issued Executive Order Number 28, establishing the gradual manumission of slaves. It was taken, almost word-for-word, from the North Carolina legislation of the previous year. No one was to be born a slave. Slaves couldn't be sold. Slaves could only be inherited at the payment of a prohibitive tax. There were generous cash incentives to people who freed their slaves. Similar payments were made to recently-freed slaves. The whole scheme was funded by the selling of Manumission Bonds.

As in the slaveholding states within the Union, the scheme was a major injection of money into the Confederacy. Slaveholders found that, by freeing their slaves, they had access to money to modernise their properties and to convert them from the growing of cotton to the growing of food crops. Economically, this became increasingly important as competition from Egyptian, Indian, and (increasingly) Australian cotton drove down the price of Confederate cotton in Europe. Slaves used their grants to buy and upgrade small farms. Given the choice between maintaining the tradition of the "peculiar institution" and having sufficient food to eat and money to spend, most Confederates opted for prosperity or, at the very least, survival.

The scheme wasn't popular everywhere. The legislature in Texas didn't cede their powers to the Provisional Administration. There was talk of further secession. "We left Mexico when we needed to. We left the United States when we wanted to. Now, maybe it's time we leave the Confederacy and go it alone," was a comment heard in many a public gathering in Texas.

Elsewhere in the Confederacy, those who had a strong emotional commitment to the institution of slavery began to look to Texas as a place where the "peculiar institution" could continue. A Louisiana planter named *Simon Legree* was the first to sell his property to purchase land in Texas to where he relocated his farm and his slaves. The fact that only 25% of his slaves actually arrived in Texas is typical of the handful of planters who attempted to relocate slaves to Texas. There were plenty of people along the route who were willing to aid a Texas-bound slave to escape. Some of those who helped were former slaves themselves. Others were whites who either opposed slavery, or who (more frequently) wanted to collect a share of the manumission money by freeing a Texas-bound slave ... or (occasionally) both.

In any event, the arrival of those who were committed to the continuance of the "peculiar institution" led to a growing rift between Texas and the Confederacy. Even though the formal secession of Texas from the Confederacy didn't take place until the escape of Emperor Maximillian from Mexico in 1867, the *de facto* separation of Texas from the Confederacy was a *fait accompli* from mid-1864 as far as policymakers in Austin, Montgomery, Washington, and Salt Lake City were concerned. Most of the Confederate army was stationed in Arkansas and Louisiana, in forts located within a few miles of the Texas state line. Most of the Union army (along with a few Deseret militia units) was similarly stationed in forts in the Protectorates, close to the Texas border.

Meanwhile, in the Union, the combined effect of the Confederate coup and the tensions with Texas had an impact on the 1864 elections. Stability was the key issue in the minds of most voters, and the electorate did not want the risks associated with either the Douglas-Johnson or Fremont-Sumner tickets. Hamlin and Lee were elected in a landslide, with a clear mandate to continue the Lincoln-Seward legacy.

11. "With malice toward none ..."

Washington, 3rd March 1865

On the day before Hannibal Hamlin was sworn in as the 17th President of what remained of the United States of America, Abraham Lincoln gave his farewell address, speaking to a gathering of invited guests in one of the public reception rooms in the White House.

He looked around at the crowd, which was much larger than the number he thought would turn up. Mary and the three boys were there, of course. So were his three stalwart political supporters over the past four years, with Hamlin and Lee taking on new responsibilities and Seward continuing on as usual in the State Department. His old friend and unofficial bodyguard Ward Hill Lamon was there. So was his old adversary Steve Douglas, as were also Fremont, Johnson, and Sumner. There were a smattering of foreign diplomats, representing Britain, France, Prussia, Deseret, and other countries. From the Confederacy, there was Edmund Kirby Smith (transferred from Salt Lake City to Washington after Benjamin joined the *junta*). Two US diplomats were also present, Thomas Meagher, Lee's successor in Montgomery, and Carl Schurz, appointed to Salt Lake City after Meagher's move. There seemed to be many more politicians and journalists present than Lincoln remembered inviting.

Lincoln began on a personal note, thanking his family and his friends for their love, care, support, and prayers over the years. He also thanked the members of his cabinet and staff. He wished the new President, Vice-President, and cabinet well.

He apologised for not preserving the Union intact. He also apologised for not ridding the continent of the evil of slavery.

One thing for which he would never apologise was for preventing the major bloodbath which would have certainly followed had hostilities broken out in 1861.

Slavery was in its final stages on this continent, he said. The number of people held as slaves, both in the Union and in the Confederacy was around 60 per cent of the number held as slaves in these areas in March of 1861. The number of slaves continues to decrease. "I have a dream that one day no person living on this continent will be judged on the colour of their skin, but on the content of their character. The day will come," he said, "when slavery will end, in both the Union and the Confederacy. I hope to see that day. I believe the person who will sit in my office at that time is alive now. The possibility is that he may even be in this room."

Wild applause erupted. Robert Lincoln blushed when he realised his two adolescent brothers were slapping his back following their father's comment.

The fragmentation of the Union was another question altogether, Lincoln said. The Union, the Confederacy, and Deseret are now three nations. Sadly, Texas may become a fourth. These nations are destined to be one but it is doubtful that this will be achieved in our lifetimes. "Let us then highly resolve, he said, that these nations, for the time being while we remain separate nations, shall continue to live in peace and friendship."

Lincoln concluded with words which, since that day, have been memorised by just about every child in American schools.

The world will little note, nor long remember what we say here, but it is rather for us to be here dedicated to the great task remaining before us. With malice toward none, with charity for all, with firmness in the right as God gives us to see the right, let us strive on to finish the work we are in, to bind up the continent's wounds, and to do all which may achieve and cherish a just and lasting peace among ourselves and with all nations; that these nations, under God, shall have a new birth of freedom—and that government of the people, by the people, for the people, shall not perish from the earth.

12. "If you prick us, do we not bleed?"

Savannah, 14th April 1865

*"Now is the winter of our discontent
Made glorious summer by this sun of York; ..."*

Judah Benjamin sat in his box in the Savannah Theatre. He had been visiting the city to meet with local officials in behalf of the Provisional Administration. Before travelling back to Montgomery in the morning, he had tickets for Shakespeare's *Richard III* tonight. In the title role was the noted actor, John Wilkes Booth, who in recent years had made the role of the villainous monarch his own. While Booth's artificial prosthetic hunchback looked far less realistic than some British Richards he'd seen, it didn't have the comic effect he'd seen in productions of *Richard III* he'd seen from some travelling companies.

Booth's opening speech continued.

*"And therefore, since I cannot prove a lover,
To entertain these fair well-spoken days,
I am determined to prove a .... to prove a ... to prove a ..."*

"Come on, Johnny, you're overacting," thought Benjamin.

"*... to prove a patriot!*" shouted Booth, whipping a Colt revolver out of the folds of his doublet and firing in the direction of Benjamin.

While the shot missed, dislodging some plaster a foot-and-a-half over Benjamin's head and creating a cloud of dust, Booth was still holding the pistol in his hand.

Booth launched into a furious denunciation of the Provisional Administration, and of Benjamin personally.

He began by condemning the Beauregard-Longstreet-Benjamin *junta* for beginning the gradual process of freeing the slaves and forever abandoning the historic Southern way of life, ... engaging in some obscene racial comments in the process. Ladies began to blush.

Then Booth became personal. He spoke of the rumours, very common in some circles, of Benjamin's homosexuality. He became graphic in his descriptions of some of the activities in which he believed Mr. Benjamin engaged. Parents covered the ears of their children.

And then Booth brought up Benjamin's Jewish heritage. He mentioned every racial and sectarian stereotype imaginable, getting increasingly vile in his comments until Benjamin could take no more. He stood and, from his box, addressed Booth and the assembled audience in the words of Shakespeare's Shylock:

"I am a Jew. Hath not a Jew eyes? hath not a Jew hands, organs, dimensions, senses, affections, passions? fed with the same food, hurt with the same weapons, subject to the same diseases, healed by the same means, warmed and cooled by the same winter and summer, as a Christian is? If you prick us, do we not bleed? if you tickle us, do we not laugh? if you poison us, do we not die? and if you wrong us, shall we not revenge? If we are like you in the rest, we will resemble you in that."

The audience stood and erupted into wild applause at Benjamin's words. Booth reddened and, in his anger, fired a shot into the air, dislodging more plaster and reminding Benjamin and the audience just who it was who held a gun.

The audience began to boo Booth.

A tomato flew through the air, splattering Booth's doublet.

Tears welled up in Booth's eyes, as other produce began to be thrown in Booth's direction.

An egg soon found its target on Booth's nose.

Booth dropped his weapon and stormed off to stage left, where two large policemen waited to arrest him.

Booth spent the rest of his life (until his death at the age of 81 during the 1918 Spanish Influenza epidemic) as a resident of the Georgia State Lunatic, Idiot, and Epileptic Asylum in Milledgeville. Booth was considered a model patient. According to a succession of Catholic chaplains at the Asylum, he was far and away the most reliable altar server among the patients. It was noted by staff that, toward the end of his life, he was far friendlier toward black, Jewish, and gay fellow-patients than he was at the beginning of his stay at the Asylum.

Booth's dramatic skills were also in demand at Milledgeville. His Friday evening recitations of great speeches from Shakespeare's plays were always well-received by patients, staff, and the more discerning townspeople alike. Booth always refused, however, to give readings from either *Richard III* or *The Merchant of Venice*.

After his experience facing down Booth, Judah Benjamin was inundated with letters, telegrams, and other messages of congratulations both from supporters and from former political adversaries. One message of support Benjamin particularly valued (and which he framed and hung on his office wall) was a cable sent from London by Abraham Lincoln.

13. Tea with the *ghillie*

At the time Abraham Lincoln read the account in The Times of London of the attempt on Judah Benjamin's life, he had only recently stepped off the ship at Southampton along with his wife Mary and his sons William and Tad. They quickly settled into their rooms in London.

After his careers as a lawyer and a political leader, Lincoln had begun a new stage of his life as a journalist and a lecturer. A number of newspapers in the United States had offered him generous fees for articles on his travels, on any notable figures he met, and on his impressions of the issues of the day overseas. As well, he soon discovered that his status in the United States led to enough of an interest in him in Britain to result in multiple invitations to speak (also, with generous fees attached) on American topics to English, Scottish, Welsh, and Irish audiences. While he was retired from political life, Abe Lincoln soon found that he wouldn't be idle.

He was also finding that many notable people in Britain were interested in inviting the Lincolns into their homes for meals and conversations. Within three months of his arrival, the family had received invitations to dinner, luncheon, and that notable British institution "high tea" from such notables as Charles Dickens, Charles Darwin, John Henry Newman, the reclusive Florence Nightingale, and a Prussian refugee named Karl Marx, who wrote dense and incomprehensible treatises on economic and political philosophy. The Lincolns became particular friends of

Father Newman and Miss Nightingale during their time in England.

They also received an invitation from Queen Victoria to dine with her and her family at the Queen's private residence on the Isle of Wight. While the Queen was still in an extended period of mourning for her husband, Prince Albert, who died four years previously, she welcomed the Lincolns warmly. Mary Lincoln became a particular friend and confidante of the Queen. Abe hit it off particularly well with the Scotsman John Brown, ostensibly the Queen's *ghillie* or "Highland Servant" (but for whom there were many whispers about his being the Queen's lover). The American statesman and the Scottish *ghillie* found they had a similar taste in long, humorous anecdotes and rural tall tales. Willie and Tad similarly enjoyed the company of the Queen's younger daughters, who were of a similar age to them, and who enjoyed flirting outrageously with the two inexperienced – and easily embarassed - young Americans. Each of the Lincolns soon became a frequent visitor to the various royal residences.

Both Willie and Tad were enrolled at Harrow. Willie was an excellent student, who excelled in his study of the classics and was an excellent public speaker, debater, and all-round sportsman. He even showed talent at the iconic English game of cricket.

Tad was less of a scholar than his brother. He was inept at sports. He had a pronounced stammer, and was self-conscious about his cleft palate and hare lip. He resolved to grow a fierce moustache when he was of an age to grow one. This was based on a suggestion from one of the Queen's daughters (the same one who taught both he and his brother how to French kiss, but not - it must be added – at the same time) that "If you grow a moustache, it will drive the ladies mad!")

Tad's one enormous talent was his ability at the piano. In a real sense, Tad let his fingers do his talking for him. Whether he was playing Mozart's *Rondo Alla Turca*, or Beethoven's *Für Elise* or *Moonlight Sonata*, or anything by Chopin, when Tad sat at the piano bench, people were overjoyed to listen.

14. Parties, flags, anthems, Alaska, and politics

The administrations of Hannibal Hamlin (1865-1869) and Robert E. Lee (1869-1873) were, in many ways, far less eventful than the Lincoln administration. The "Velvet Divorce" between the Union and the Confederacy was bearing fruit in far friendlier relations between North and South than had ever been the case in living knowledge. (No one was ever sure who first coined the term "Velvet Divorce". William Seward and Judah Benjamin were both suggested, as were such overseas statesmen as Gladstone, Disraeli, and Bismarck.)

The voluntary liberation of slaves continued at a rapid pace, both in the Union and in the Confederacy. The economies of both the Union and the Confederacy boomed, particularly as a result of the injection of the "manumission money" into the economy. The Beauregard-Longstreet-Benjamin *junta* in Montgomery began planning for a gradual transition back to democratic, civilian rule. Further west, Deseret prospered and, in many ways, began to show signs of positive social and political change. The strongest area of concern and headaches for policymakers (whether in Washington, Montgomery, or Salt Lake City) was Texas, but this statement would hold true from the Hamlin administration until the Great War.

During the late 1860s and early 1870s, the three political parties which even today dominate American politics began to appear: the Progressives, the Patriots, and the Populists. While they first appeared in the Union, these three parties also suited the Confederacy when it made its transition back to civilian government in the 1880s and Deseret when it transitioned to secular government at the same time. At Reunification, the Union, Confederate, and Deseret organisations of each of these parties simply merged with each other.

The Progressives sought to continue the legacy of Lincoln. They were essentially moderate in their approach to economic issues and progressive in their promotion of an inclusive society and their opposition to corruption. They championed the cause of freed slaves and sought to ensure that a former slave was a full citizen with all of the corresponding rights and responsibilities. They also championed the cause of immigrants, regardless of their country of origin or their religious persuasion.

The Patriots (or "Pats") essentially represented the interests of "old money" and those heavily-propertied families who possessed "old money". Through the nineteenth and early twentieth centuries, their Presidential and Vice-Presidential candidates had surnames that suggested ancestors among the Mayflower pilgrims, Tidewater Virginia planters, or Hudson Valley Knickerbocker Dutch. The Pats were the most economically conservative of the three parties, but they didn't exhibit the hostility toward Blacks, Jews, Catholics, or immigrants showed by the Populists at their worst. (Neither did they embrace their cause with the enthusiasm of the Progressives at their best.)

The Populists (or "Pops") opposed the privileges of "old money" traditionally supported by the Pats, but they also opposed any attempt at economic and social equality for anyone who wasn't white, native-born, and Protestant. The Populists were once described by Dorothy Parker as being "somewhere to the left of Robin Hood on economic issues and somewhere to the right of Attila the Hun on almost everything else".

While the Progressives dominated national politics (in the Union, in the Confederacy, and in Deseret before Reunification; and in the USA after Reunification), there were still enough support for the other parties (particularly in three-candidate races) to make politics interesting, at least until recent years.

Will Rogers once summed up the two smaller parties by saying that the parties' nicknames gave the best clue for how to deal with their politicians: "With the Pats, you just *pat* them on the head and compliment them on their breeding, their tailoring, and their table manners. With the Pops, you just *pop* open a bottle of whiskey with them and pretend to laugh at their jokes."

Particularly as a result of William Jennings Bryan making an issue of Al Smith's Catholicism in the 1924 election and decimating the Populists' support as a result, the Pops are now no longer as rabidly anti-Catholic as they once were. From the 1940s onwards, it was no longer possible to find copies of **Foxe's Book of Martyrs** or the **Awful Disclosures of Maria Monk** for sale at the booktables at Populist Party meetings, although the **Protocols of the**

Elders of Zion was still openly available through the mid-1960s. (The Pops even ran Senator Fidel Castro from the state of American Caribbean – a Catholic, albeit a spectacularly non-practicing one - as a presidential candidate three times in the 1960s and 1970s.)

Nevertheless, there was (and is) still an enduring racist and antisemitic streak among many supporters of the Populist Party. (The racist dimension was exhibited most dramatically when Castro's 1972 Vice-Presidential candidate, New Jersey Congressman Charles Sandman, described the involvement of US troops in the marathon South African Civil War as "white boys dying in a black man's war".)

Over the decades, the feeling developed that the Pops essentially functioned as the political home for the disaffected and the alienated. (For example, research in the 1990s showed that the one demographic most inclined to vote for Populist Party candidates was that of divorced men who were still single even though their ex-wives had remarried.) In the 2004 presidential election, votes for the Populists were described by a journalist for the *New York Times* as "inarticulate protest votes cast by the perpetually pissed-off".

A commentator for the *Wall Street Journal* once wrote that the historical reputations of the minor parties, coupled with the desire of most Americans to view themselves as "comfortably middle class", had the effect of creating long-standing stigmas for the minor parties and their supporters. "Americans don't like regarding themselves as 'old money', even if they are, so they resist voting for the Pats, even if they like the Pats' policies. Similarly, many people potentially attracted by the Pops' policies don't vote for them because they choose not to view themselves as unstable, unsuccessful, angry, or a 'loser'."

In recent decades, both the Pats and the Pops have found it increasingly difficult to field strong candidates for national elections. During the 2008 election, a stand-up comedian described the typical Patriot ticket as "a retired Major General running for President with a former District Attorney running for Veep, neither of whom you've ever heard of," with the typical Populist ticket consisting of "a second-term congressman running for President with a retired police chief as his running-mate, both of whom you've probably heard of but wish you hadn't".

Back to the nineteenth century, it was during this time of the Hamlin and Lee administrations where much of the terminology and symbolism of the three nations were fixed for the bulk of the sixty-five years between Sumter and Reunification.

North of the border, while the name "United States of America" was still the official, constitutional term for those states which didn't secede, an informal consensus soon developed that the phrases "United States of America", "United States", or "USA" were only to be used for the nation prior to the secessions of the Confederacy and Deseret, as well as for whatever reunited nation would be established at some time in the future. The group of states which did not secede was generally referred to as "the Union".

It was during this time as well that some tunes which were used as unofficial national anthems in the Union, in the Confederacy, and in Deseret each assumed some official standing.

In Deseret, the Mormon hymn "Come, come, ye saints" with its refrain "All is well, all is well!" had been used as an unofficial national anthem since secession. The rollicking "Dixie" had a similar role in the Confederacy. William Clayton's hymn and Daniel Decatur Emmett's minstrel song were both given official status as national anthems in the late 1860s.

A few years later, "The Battle Hymn of the Republic" received a similar status in the Union. Its writer, Julia Ward Howe, wrote the hymn in 1861 anticipating a war between the Union and the Confederacy. While the war was avoided, the martial imagery in the hymn became part of the culture, to the extent that "The Battle Hymn of the Republic" was recognised as the Union's national anthem late in the Lee administration.

Comparing the origins and the style of the three anthems, many Confederates noted gleefully to their friends from Deseret and the Union that "You Yankees have national anthems that y'all can sing in church, while we have an anthem we can *dance to*."

While the Union kept the same flag that was used by the US since the Revolutionary War, and while the Beehive flag used by the Territory of Utah was kept by Deseret, the Confederacy felt the need for a more distinctive flag. It was General Beauregard himself who designed a flag incorporating a blue saltire on a red background with a pattern of white stars on the satire. This flag was recognised as the Confederacy's national flag in 1868.

Moving from national symbolism to actual politics, William Seward proved to be one of the Union's great Secretaries of State, guiding international relations both with the powers of Europe and with the Union's neighbours in North America in both the Lincoln and Hamlin administrations. His one major disappointment was the Senate's rejection of the 1867 proposal that the Union purchase Alaska from Russia. (This had the effect of keeping Alaska in Russian hands into the twentieth century, providing a refuge for some members of the Romanoff dynasty after the 1917 Revolution, at least until Tsar Alexei was invited back as a limited, constitutional monarch after Stalin was overthrown following the 1933 Food Riots.)

Seward's resignation was only prevented by an all-night session of persuasion on the part of Hamlin and Lee, assisted by telegrams from Confederate and Deseret political leaders, a cable sent from London by Abe Lincoln, and large quantities of Lee's best bourbon. Seward completed his service as Secretary of State at the end of the Hamlin administration. Lee appointed Thomas Meagher as Seward's successor, who served during the Lee and Blaine administrations.

In the Union, the tradition of one-term Presidents begun by Martin Van Buren continued for the remainder of the 19th century. (The sixty-four year series of one-term Presidents from 1837 to 1901 has since been well overtaken by the eighty-four year series of one-term Presidents from the end of Al Smith's second term in 1933 to the present.) Candidates from the Progressive Party dominated the presidential elections against mostly lacklustre opposition from the Pats and the Pops. At the 1872 election, James G. Blaine, Speaker of the House of Representatives, was elected to succeed Lee. Blaine was succeeded by Rutherford B. Hayes in 1876, who was succeeded by James A Garfield in 1880. (Vice-President Chester A. Arthur served as Acting President for six months early in Garfield's presidency, while Garfield was recovering from a gunshot wound received during an assassination attempt. Garfield credited "a bossy Englishwoman hired by my wife to ride roughshod over my incompetent doctors" with saving his life.)

Grover Cleveland from the Pats succeeded Garfield in 1884. (Because of Vice-President Arthur's poor health, the Progressives nominated Blaine for a second term as President after eight years in private life.) The Progressives returned to power with the election of Benjamin Harrison, who defeated Cleveland in his attempt for a second term in 1888.

In the Confederacy, the *junta* handed over power to a restored civilian government in 1880. A new constitution provided for a five-year term (with no stated term limits) for the President. Judah Benjamin, the one civilian member of the Executive, was in poor health. The two generals were also reluctant to put themselves forward to lead a civilian government. Edmund Kirby-Smith, the former soldier and diplomat, was persuaded to leave his position as a mathematics professor just over the border in Sewanee, Tennessee, to serve for a single term as the Confederacy's first civilian President since Jefferson Davis. He was succeeded by the two military members of the junta's executive (by then civilians) for a term each, Beauregard in 1885 and Longstreet in 1890. As in the Union, each of the three represented the dominant Progressive Party, with the Pats and the Pops offering only token opposition. The Confederate branch of the Pats frequently contemplated inviting Jeff Davis to return to the Confederacy as the party's leader, but he chose to remain in his Canadian exile until his death in 1889. By 1895, the Confederacy (and the Confederate Progressive Party in particular) was looking for younger leadership than that provided by the men of the 1860s.

One major political change that took place during this period was in the beginning of women's suffrage. The right of women to vote was first affirmed by the Wyoming Territory in the Union in 1869. In the following year, women became voters in the Commonwealth of Deseret. Confederate women's right to vote became law at the handover of power from the *junta* to civilian government in 1880, with the right of women in the Protectorates to vote coming a year later in 1881, the same year in which women in the ironically-named Isle of Man in the Irish Sea became the first European women to vote. Through the 1870s and the early 1880s, some states and territories in the Union affirmed the right of women to vote, but women's suffrage only became a reality throughout the Union shortly before James Garfield handed the keys of the White House to Grover Cleveland after the 1884 election. This was due in large part to the active lobbying of the convalescent President Garfield on the subject by his activist English nurse. In Texas, however, the right to vote was restricted to white, male, Gentile landowners until after Texas's defeat in the Great War.

15. "God bless us, every one!" (part 1)

Edgbaston Oratory, Birmingham, England, June 1867

Tad Lincoln sat at the upright piano in the refectory at the Edgbaston Oratory in Birmingham, in the English midlands. He and his family were dinner guests of the Oratory's superior, the noted theologian and convert Father John Henry Newman.

Tad didn't plan to play the piano but his mother boasted greatly of his abilities on the piano over the spicy Mulligatawny soup, the Atlantic cod, and the sweet Rhine wine. During the pause before the next course, Father Newman invited Tad to play the piano if he wished. Without his sheet music, he played two pieces he knew by heart, Beethoven's *Moonlight Sonata*, followed by Mozart's *Rondo Alla Turca*.

When he concluded, loud applause erupted from his parents, his brother, and the various clerics. In the conversation over the rare roast beef and the French claret, Father Newman asked him if he planned to further his musical studies.

"Yes, sir. I'm not much of a scholar, really. Willie's the scholar and the sportsman. He's bound for Oxford and a few brilliant years of classics and cricket. After Harrow, I'm planning to study music in Paris or Vienna or possibly Italy, and then make a career out of my music if I can." (In fact, Tad was being overly self-deprecating in his comments and, in this self-deprecation, demonstrated the extent to which he and his brother were becoming authentic *Englishmen*. Once Tad discovered the extent of his musical abilities, he became far more confident – and far less inept – in the classroom, on the playing-field, and in social situations.) "My parents' friend Miss Nightingale has a number of friends on the Continent who are musicians and she thinks they can help locate a suitable teacher for me." Newman nodded sagely.

Mary Lincoln complimented her hosts on the quality of the meal. Father Newman replied, "On a typical evening, we enjoy much simpler fare but, then, we don't always entertain an international statesman and a future concert virtuoso."

Abe complimented the wines, adding, "In America, I never consumed much strong drink, but there it was mostly the rough corn whiskies of the frontier. Here, with the elegant wines of the Continent, the cleansing ales of England, and the mystical spirits of Scotland and Ireland, my teetotal days seem to have come to an end." The assembled company shared Abe's laughter.

Willie was involved in discussing some obscure point of philosophy with a few of the younger priests. One of the most animated participants in the discussion was a short, slight cleric, only recently ordained, who walked into the room with a pronounced limp, aided by a walking stick.

Mary Lincoln said to Father Newman, "The young man with the walking stick appears healthy now, but I have the feeling he wasn't always so. That was also the case with my boys."

Newman replied, "Yes, *Father Cratchit* had very poor health as a child. It was only when his father's employer realised the extent of the family's poverty and young *Tim's* poor health that they were able to afford proper medical care for *Tim*, and a decent education for all the children. Yes and before you ask, our *Father Cratchit* is also Mr. Dickens's *Tiny Tim*. When he told the family's story, he asked the family's permission to use their real names, in tribute (particularly) to *Tim's* father and his commitment to their well-being. *Tim* was once embarrassed by this, but now he finds people's reactions to his identity to be a source of amusement mostly."

The meal continued, through a rich fruit pudding, a sharp Stilton cheese, and a decanter of port. Newman invited his guests to join the priests for Compline in the chapel before they returned to their lodgings. "But first, he said, a toast! *Father Cratchit*, may I ask you to propose your usual toast?"

"With pleasure, Father Newman. ... May we all stand for the toast. …. God bless us every one!"

They all replied, draining their glasses of port, "God bless us every one!"

16. Maximillian I and his successors

It is an ongoing cliché of movie westerns that "the day a stranger rode into town" was the beginning of high drama. On the same afternoon in May of 1867, strangers rode into town in two cities in western North America.

In neither case, did they ride in on a horse. One arrived alone and unheralded in Salt Lake City on a Wells Fargo stagecoach. The other arrived in a fishing boat at the port of Brownsville, Texas, accompanied by two generals and greeted by a delegation of politicians and a brass band.

The man coming in to Brownsville by fishing boat was Maximillian I, brother of the Austrian Emperor and himself the recently-deposed Emperor of Mexico. The short-lived Mexican Empire was at an end. President Benito Juárez was re-establishing his authority. There was a price on the former Emperor's head, and on the heads of General Miguel Miramón and General Tomás Mejía. Empress Carlota returned to Europe on an unsuccessful mission to muster European support for her husband. The Emperor and his generals clambered onto an old fishing boat and headed north.

Brownsville was the first port outside of Mexican territory. The Emperor and his men were unsure about who was really ruling in Brownsville. Whether Texas was still part of the Confederacy or not was a disputed point.

As the boat finally left Mexican waters and approached the Texas coastline, Maximillian saw a crowd of men, mostly in suits. A brass band was playing badly. As the boat drew closer to the shore, Maximillian could make out the tune which was being mangled was the *Volkshymne*, the national anthem of the Austrian Empire, using a tune by Joseph Haydn. He realised that the men in suits were there to greet him, and not for any hostile purpose.

As the three men disembarked at the pier, the crowd rushed up to them. One short man, dressed in a somewhat more expensive-looking suit than the others, approached Maximillian and declared loudly "Your Imperial Majesty, I welcome you on behalf of the people of Texas. By the authority of the government and the legislature of Texas, I offer you the office of Emperor of Texas. Do you accept this office, sir?"

Maximillian was flustered. He offered his hand to the stranger, to shake it. After they shook hands, the short man knelt and kissed Maximillian's hand. He arose and shouted "Long live the Emperor of Texas!"

The crowd thundered, "Long live the Emperor of Texas!"

The band returned to mangling the *Volkshymne*.

Maximillian whispered to his generals, "So much for returning to Vienna."

The Emperor and his generals proceeded to Austin where he took residence in the Governor's Mansion, which soon became known as the Emperor's Palace. He sent for the Empress to come back to the New World from her unsuccessful attempts to find European support.

His first official act was to issue a formal decree stating that, as he had accepted the throne of Emperor of Texas at the invitation of the people's representatives, he now officially declared the secession of Texas from the Confederacy.

He soon learned that the only things he needed to do were to, firstly, to officially ratify decisions by the small cabal of politicians and businessmen who actually decided things and, secondly and most importantly, to look impressive in a dress uniform, thus giving a veneer of respectability on formal occasions to the Texan kleptocracy and nepotocracy. While he found it distasteful, particularly when he had to deal with the coarse, oily *Simon Legree*, who managed to wangle himself into the important-sounding (and probably overly well-paid, and with minimal actual work involved) job of *"First Deputy Inspector of Public Projects"* (or something like that), he realised that dealing with the likes of *Legree* was still infinitely preferable to the prospect of facing Juárez's firing squad.

When Maximillian I died of malaria in 1875, the Texan politicians requested Emperor Franz-Joseph in Vienna to appoint another Hapsburg to sit on the Texan throne.

A system soon developed by which, whenever the Texan throne fell vacant, the Emperor would appoint a minor Hapsburg to reign in Austin. The Texan requirements for an Emperor were that he speak passable English, look impressive in a dress uniform, and have no interest in getting involved in the details of day-to-day politics. It went without saying that the Emperor needed to be sufficiently amoral to tolerate slavery, the corruption of the Texan oligarchs, and (after 1882) polygamy.

The main Viennese requirement for the man they sent to Texas as Emperor was that his behaviour constituted a sufficient long-term embarrassment to the Emperor to get him out of Europe permanently.

Thus, we have the line of minor Hapsburgs who reigned in Austin from 1867 until 1917.

After Maximillian died, the next Emperor of Texas was *Ignaz I*. He died in 1881 after being shot by the jealous husband of one of his mistresses.

The next Emperor was *Alois I*. He died in 1885 after being shot by the jealous wife of one of his court favourites.

In 1893, the next Emperor, *Alois II*, was also shot and killed. In his case, it was by the angry father of a fourteen-year-old girl whom he seduced.

Ignaz II was shot and killed by his own empress in 1900. No one really knew why, but there was plenty of speculation, all of which was lurid to the extreme.

None of the regicides were ever brought to trial. It was felt that a criminal trial in a court of law, even in an easily controlled Texan court, could prove to be an embarrassment to the Empire.

Maximillian II was considered, far and away, the best of the Hapsburg Emperors of Texas. Franz-Joseph sent him to Texas for the comparatively minor embarrassment of heavy gambling debts. He was uncomfortable with the systemic corruption of the Texan system and fought constantly with the political and business establishment throughout his ten-year reign. He was the first emperor since *Maximillian I* to live in a comfortably monogamous relationship with his Empress. *Maximillian II* died in 1910 when he was swept overboard from ***The Titanic*** while assisting women and children into lifeboats.

Maximillian III represented a return to the usual pattern. Even though he had a far lower sex drive than many of his predecessors and (thus) avoided the typical vices of most Texan Emperors, he was a glutton and an alcoholic. He led Texas into the Great War on the side of the Central Powers, and died in exile in Japan after the defeat of Texas.

But, back to the early years of the Texan Empire, the comparatively small number of slaves in a slave-based agricultural economy led to gangs of Texan bandits raiding communities and settlements over the borders seeking to bring slaves back to Texas. They raided communities in Louisiana and Arkansas looking for freed blacks to enslave. They raided communities in the Protectorates seeking Cherokees, Choctaws and other Native Americans to enslave. They raided communities in Mexico seeking Mexican slaves. (When these raids on Mexico became common, Maximillian's two Mexican generals decided New Orleans was a safer place for them than Austin, so they quickly and quietly slipped out of the country by a fishing boat similar to the one in which they arrived.)

At this time, the bulk of the Confederate, Union, Deseret, and Mexican armies were stationed within fifty miles of the border with Texas, seeking to prevent Texan bandits from enslaving innocent people. In the Protectorates, where Union and Deseret forces patrolled the borders with Texas, many a military reputation was made. The Virginians Thomas Jackson (given the name "Stone-Wall" as a tribute by a Cherokee chief) and J.E.B. Stuart, along with the Midwesterners Ulysses S. Grant and William T. Sherman, led hardened troops who did their best to protect isolated communities from criminal raiders.

From 1867 until the beginning of the Great War, units of the Union, Confederate, and Deseret armies regularly fought deadly battles against raiders from Texas. As well, the government of Texas exercised strict controls on its borders, with few people from outside the Empire being allowed to visit Texas, and even fewer (other than the elite) being allowed to travel beyond the Empire's borders. These closed borders prompted Prime Minister Benjamin Disraeli to declare in London, in 1878, during a debate on North American affairs in the House of Lords, that "an Iron Curtain has descended on the North American continent. Behind that line lie all the cities and towns of that once great state of Texas: Houston, Dallas, Fort Worth, San Antonio, Austin, El Paso."

Nevertheless, from the beginning there was one Texan commodity that many people outside Texas wanted: beef. After 1901, there was a second commodity: oil. Because of those two Texan products, there was a general reluctance on the part of Texas's neighbours in the Union, the Confederacy, Deseret, and Mexico to stand up to the Texan oligarchs with too much vigor.

17. "Capisce, I think." (part 1)

In 1869, Abe and Mary Lincoln decided it was time to travel again. They had been outside the United States for four years. They had seen much of England, Wales, Scotland, Ireland, and France. They had become comfortably well-off through Abe's writing and public lectures.

They and their sons had made good friends in England, including such notable people as Florence Nightingale and John Henry Newman, not to mention the Queen and her family. (Abe was particularly friendly with the Queen's *ghillie* - and probable lover – John Brown, with whom he shared a similar sense of humour.)

Willie was at Oxford, studying classics, playing cricket, taking instruction to become a Roman Catholic, and was thinking about studying for the priesthood after taking his degree.

Tad (who now wanted to be known as Thomas to all but his family) was in his last year at Harrow, and had arranged to study piano with a teacher in Vienna in the following year. He was a reasonable student and a competent rower. Whenever he was away from school, he grew an attempt at a moustache to cover up his hare lip.

Both boys had standing invitations to stay with Miss Nightingale and with Father Newman whenever they wished. The younger members of the Royal Family frequently invited both Willie and Tad to stay with them, particularly during holidays at their Scottish residence at Balmoral.

Abe and Mary decided it was time to see the rest of the world. In the summer of 1869, they embarked from Southampton to Italy. While avoiding areas of fighting, during the closing stages of the conflict for Italian unification, they managed to see the historic sights of Rome, Venice, Pisa, and Florence. They had an audience with Pius IX, lunch with General Garibaldi, and dinner with King Victor Emmanuel (without mentioning to any of them that they were meeting the others).

They sailed onwards, seeing the ancient sights of Greece, Constantinople, the Holy Land, and Egypt. They sailed through the Suez Canal only a few months after it had been opened for the use of ships. In India, they marvelled at the Taj Mahal, among other sights. From Calcutta, they set sail for Australia in August of 1870.

Meanwhile, Thomas (having finally shed the childhood nickname, Tad) was spending the final weeks of the summer at the home of Florence Nightingale. After his final term at Harrow, he spent the first part of the summer at Balmoral (and managed to lose his virginity), and two weeks in Birmingham where the newly converted William (who had ceased to be "Willie" at the time he went up to Oxford) was spending the whole summer with Father Newman, *Father Cratchit*, and the other priests. Before travelling to Vienna and beginning his life as a serious musician, Thomas spent the late summer at Miss Nightingale's home.

Normally, he spent the morning practicing the piano in the main drawing room while the invalid Miss Nightingale (bedridden since shortly after returning from the Crimea) listened to him play as she remained in her bed with the door of her bedroom opened. He'd hear the periodic burst of applause and the occasional "Bravo!" from Miss Nightingale's room.

But, on one otherwise unremarkable Tuesday morning, as Thomas worked his way through a particularly difficult Chopin nocturne, he looked up and saw Miss Nightingale. She was out of bed, groomed, dressed, and walking unassisted. "Well, Miss Nightingale," said Thomas, "it's my turn to say 'Bravo!'"

Later that same day, in Birmingham, William had a serious talk with Father Newman and *Father Cratchit* about his plans. He had one more year at Oxford before taking his degree. William was thinking of applying for the priesthood through an English diocese and hoping to study at the English College in Rome, and then to serve as a priest in England.

Newman thought for a while and said, "William, you'd be a far more useful priest back in America. Here in England, you'll be one more middle-class convert priest struggling to serve congregations made up mainly of Irish labourers and their families. Return to America. You'll have a far better ministry than you will here in Britain."

"Shall I study at the North American College when I go to Rome, then?"

"How is your proficiency in Italian?" asked *Tim Cratchit*. "Can you buy some bread and cheese, or a bottle of wine, in Italian? Can you read an Italian newspaper? Can you order a coffee in an Italian café? Can you ask for directions in an Italian city?"

"No. My Latin is excellent, my Greek is good, my German is reasonable, and my French is essentially comical, but my Italian is non-existent."

"Well then," said Newman, "here's a plan. We'll need to get you related to an American diocese. As your last place of residence in America was in Washington, I'd suggest Baltimore. You should start your seminary training in some English-speaking country. I'd suggest Maynooth in Ireland. You liked your time at Maynooth, didn't you, *Tim*?"

"Yes."

Newman continued, "After two years there, you can go to Rome. By that time Garibaldi's army should have ceased making nuisances of themselves on the outskirts of Rome. In the meantime you can learn some basic Italian. Capisce?"

"Capisce, I think."

18. The arrival of "young Joseph"

On the same day in May of 1867 as Maximillian and his generals disembarked from the fishing boat at Brownsville, a thirty-four year-old man got off the Wells Fargo stagecoach at the company's Salt Lake City depot.

Joseph Smith III was the eldest surviving of Joseph Smith, Jr., the founder of the Latter-Day Saints. He was eleven when his father was murdered by a mob in Illinois. While some of the Mormons wanted "young Joseph" to succeed his father as the "President, Prophet, Seer, and Revelator" of the church, the majority chose to follow Brigham Young west to Deseret.

A smaller group remained in Illinois and nearby states and established a "Reorganized" Latter-Day Saints Church, rejecting many of the more eccentric beliefs and practices of the Deseret group, including polygamy. When "young Joseph" was considered old enough, he was received by the Reorganized church as its leader.

And now, he was entering the heartland of the larger Mormon group. He wanted to unite the Midwestern and Deseret wings of the LDS movement into a single whole. More importantly, he wanted to unite the two factions into a single whole without polygamy.

He knew that he needed to take a longer view. Brigham Young was well-entrenched in power. He knew how to use his power and was not above the use of violence. In response to the power exerted by Young, patience and tact were the key weapons in "young Joseph's" armoury.

He checked into a rooming-house neat the Wells-Fargo depot and arranged for water for a hot bath. Tomorrow, he'll pay a courtesy call on "Brother Brigham".

"Young Joseph's" tact and patience paid off. Brigham Young wasn't threatened by the son of his predecessor. In fact, he saw the younger man's journey from Illinois to Deseret as an affirmation of his authority. Brother Brigham was getting older. He needed a successor. "Young Joseph" seemed intelligent. Let's give him some responsibilities and see what he'll do with it.

"Young Joseph" was well-received by the people of Deseret. He soon sent back to Illinois for his wife and children. Those Mormons who remembered his father were pleased to see the younger Smith in a role of responsibility. Those who resented the autocratic style of Brother Brigham were pleased to see a person in a leadership role with a more open style. Those who supported Brother Brigham's leadership were happy about the respect that "Young Joseph" showed to the senior leader. "Young Joseph" ascended rapidly up the Mormon hierarchy. The "Reorganised" strand of Latter-Day Saints living in the Midwest soon merged with the larger group in Deseret, even if most were happy to remain in Illinois and Iowa. As "Young Joseph" never practiced polygamy, he was used by Brother Brigham as the acceptable face of the Latter-Day Saints in relations with the Union and the Confederacy.

And, as it turned out, Deseret's "peculiar institution" was beginning to show as many cracks in it as the

Confederacy's. More and more Mormons were questioning the wisdom of plural marriage. The fact that a rich man could marry as many wives as he could support meant that many other young men were forced to remain bachelors. Middle-aged men found that the only unmarried women in their communities were either elderly widows, on one hand, or giggling teenagers, on the other. The fact that these men were also, according to Mormon practice, expected to be teetotallers added to their frustrations by removing one of the traditional avenues by which long-term bachelors dealt with their frustrations.

As a result, when Brother Brigham died of cholera in 1877 and was rapidly succeeded by "Young Joseph", now 44, one of the main questions asked around Deseret was "When will he end polygamy and how will he do it?"

"Young Joseph" took his time. His first actions had nothing to do with polygamy. He separated the civil government of Deseret from the government of the LDS Church. The President of the Church was no longer automatically the President of the Commonwealth. Free elections were called in 1878. Non-Mormons had the same right to a vote as Mormons. (Since 1870, women had the same right to a vote as men.) Out of a field of seven candidates, "Young Joseph" won the Presidency easily. While the same individual ("Young Joseph") remained as President of both Church and State at the time, the linkage was no longer automatic. "Young Joseph" remained as head of the government of Deseret by popular vote. His support among non-Mormons was as high as it was among Mormons. After "Young Joseph's" death in 1914, different individuals held these roles in Church and State.

In 1880, a process was approved by both the LDS Church and the Commonwealth by which a family practicing plural marriages could choose to end the arrangement. The group of plural wives would decide among themselves, by consensus, which of them would remain with the husband. In most cases, the "sister wives" would decide that the wife who remained with the husband was the one who had the least options outside the marriage. Those with supportive families, or independent incomes, or better employment prospects, or who seemed the most generally "marriageable" a second time around were less likely to remain. Normally, the "sister wife" who was happiest to remain in the marriage was the one who remained.

At the same time, the Commonwealth and the LDS Church co-operated to set up a welfare scheme to assist in feeding, housing, educating, and providing job training for former plural wives whose marriages ended. The scheme was financed by selling "monogamy bonds", similar to the "manumission bonds" sold in the Union and Confederacy.

This was the beginning of Deseret's famed "cradle-to-grave" social welfare programme, which was in full swing by the time of the Great War. When similar social welfare schemes began in Europe's Nordic countries in the 20th century, many social commentators referred to their nations adopting "a Mormon welfare state".

Two years later, in 1882, the Commonwealth and the Church announced that no new plural marriages would be sanctioned.

Two years after that, in 1884, the final announcement was made. All existing plural marriages would be dissolved within three years. The "sister wives" in each marriage would decide which one of their number remained with their husband and which ones didn't.

While there was some resistance to these changes, mostly in the decision of some polygamists to migrate to Texas (where the government indicated an openness to allowing polygamy), the vast majority of Mormons were (quite frankly) relieved to see the end of polygamy, in a similar way to the way that most southerners, in both the Union and the Confederacy, were relieved to see the end of slavery.

The end of polygamy, the separation of Church and State, and the beginning of Deseret's iconic social welfare system were not the only profound changes brought to Deseret by "Young Joseph". For one thing, within a month after taking control, "Young Joseph" quickly reversed Brother Brigham's ruling that only white people could serve as priests in the LDS Church.

But it was as much a shift in attitude and culture as it was in formal policies. Brother Brigham's long-standing social conservatism inspired resentment among many of the people of Deseret. "Young Joseph" represented a move back to his father's profound optimism regarding human nature and God's generosity. The Latter-Day Saints' traditional practice of abstinence from alcohol and caffeine was relaxed, and was treated as health-related advice rather than as a firm standard that divided the practicing from the non-practicing. The distinctive writings, beliefs, and rituals of the Mormons were treated less as literal fact and more as metaphors containing spiritual and ethical truth for those who sought moral guidance.

While the Mormon influence continued strongly, and provided a sense of social cohesion, increasingly many non-Mormons chose to make their homes in Deseret because of the warm and welcoming community spirit. By the end of the nineteenth century, Deseret was seen as being as much the home of a diverse population as its neighbours in the Union and the Confederacy.

19. "The Sage of Hobart Town"

When Abe and Mary Lincoln disembarked from their ship at the port of Hobart in late September of 1870, the last stage of the voyage – from Fremantle in Western Australia to Hobart on the Australian island of Tasmania – had been particularly rough. Both had been ill for much of the voyage. The prospect of dry land ... dry, stable land ... was appealing. Hobart looked like a good place to spend a few months and recover. The sight of the massive Mount Wellington forming a backdrop to the small port looked majestic. They decided to find some rooms and stay for a few months, spending at least the rest of the Southern Hemisphere spring and some of the summer.

The "few months" turned into almost six years. They found comfortable and spacious rooms close to the centre of town. While the locals recognised who they were, they didn't seem overawed by them. While Mary missed the formality of England, her husband enjoyed the classically Australian "G'day, Abe" from acquaintances and strangers, and particularly from the children.

They soon fell into a comfortable routine. Mary soon became busy with her involvements in many charitable committees, working to provide books for local libraries, teachers for local schools, and staff for the local hospital. Mary also wrote letters, letters to her great London friends Queen Victoria and Florence Nightingale, and, above all, letters to her three sons: Thomas studying music in Vienna and beginning his career as a concert pianist,

William at seminary in Maynooth and then in Rome, and Robert forging ahead in his law practice in Chicago.

Meanwhile, Abe decided it was time for him to write his memoirs. As a result, while it was published by Scribner's in New York, Abe's account of his political career, his struggles with avoiding a fratricidal bloodbath in the 1860s, and his opinions of the noted people they met in Britain and Europe, was written in the study of the Lincolns' apartment overlooking the Derwent River in Tasmania.

They gravitated toward the local gathering of Quakers, or to give their proper name, the Religious Society of Friends. Over the years, the Lincolns had been religious "seekers" of a sort which was very common in the United States. They had great respect for religious faith. They frequently attended worship, with faith communities of all sorts, but hesitated to join any particular church. This was also their pattern in Britain, attending congregations of the Church of England, the Roman Catholics, the Methodists, the Quakers, and any others as they felt they wished. In Tasmania, they felt particularly at home among the Quakers. By the time they had been in Hobart for two years, they even took the step of asking that their names be recorded as "Quakers by Convincement", a request unanimously granted by the Meeting.

But their membership in the Quakers was not the end of the Lincolns' involvement with Hobart's religious life. Churches of other denominations, particularly the Methodists and Congregationalists, frequently invited Abe to be a guest speaker in their services, most often for the second service on a Sunday, held in the late afternoon or early evening. Other denominations for whom it wasn't possible to invite Abe as a speaker in worship – Anglicans, Catholics, and Hobart's small but active Jewish community - still invited him as an after-dinner speaker for special events. Because Abe's messages were always simple, understandable, practical, filled with compassion, void of sectarian bias, and always mercifully brief, Abe's services as a lay preacher were always well in demand. One Sunday evening, the minister at the Davey Street Congregational Church introduced Abe as "the Sage of Hobart Town". The name stuck.

And so it continued for five-and-a-half years, until the evening in February of 1876 when Abe and Mary were walking home from a service at Wesley Church in Melville Street. Earlier in the week, Abe had received a telegram from Mr. Scribner that he had received the final draft of Abe's memoirs and was ready to publish.

As well, Mary received letters from each of her three sons. Thomas decided he wanted to live in New York, giving concerts in cities in North America. William, already a deacon, had been appointed to a parish in Baltimore with plans for his ordination as a priest there in June. Robert had been approached by the President to take up a diplomatic post in Salt Lake City.

Mary said, "Abe, perhaps it's time to go home."

20. "Capisce, I think." (part 2)

New York, 2nd July 1881

Five years later, in the summer of 1881, Abe and Mary Lincoln were living in Philadelphia. It was close enough to Baltimore, where William, now a priest, was serving as the private secretary to the Archbishop. It was also close enough to New York, where Thomas was living when he wasn't touring and giving piano recitals. It was also close enough to Washington to see Robert on those rare occasions when he visited the capital to report to the President and the Secretary of State on diplomatic concerns in London, where he was posted after spending two years as a diplomat in Salt Lake City and two years in Montgomery.

In Philadelphia, the Lincolns also were busy in the life of the Arch Street Quaker Meeting, as well as with the committees of a variety of charities, particularly those assisting former slaves. When Thomas gave one of his frequent concerts in Philadelphia, they were always involved in hosting parties for Philadelphia's large community of musical enthusiasts. As well, whenever William travelled to Philadelphia with his Archbishop for a meeting, Abe and Mary frequently provided hospitality for a variety of black-clad ecclesiastical gentlemen.

But on this Saturday afternoon, Abe and Mary were in New York to meet a close friend. Florence Nightingale had sailed from England to New York to give a series of lectures on her nursing experiences in the Crimea and on her theories on public health and hygiene. After her prolonged convalescent had ended eleven years ago, she began lecturing across Britain, Ireland, and Europe, making up for lost time. In her frequent letters to Mary, she kept saying that she wanted to visit North America. Now, she was finally giving a lecture tour visiting New York, Boston, Montréal, Toronto, Buffalo, Pittsburgh, Philadelphia, Baltimore, Washington, Richmond, Charleston, and Savannah.

Abe and Mary left their suite in the Astor House Hotel to have luncheon with Florence at Delmonico's. Thomas would meet them there as well, as well as a young lady named Emma with whom Thomas had recently been keeping company. In his last letter, Thomas mentioned that Emma was a writer.

When they arrived at Delmonico's, Florence was waiting for them, as were Thomas (sporting a fiercely elegant moustache) accompanied by a strikingly beautiful young woman. Thomas introduced his guest. "Mother, father, may I present my friend Miss Emma Lazarus?"

As always, Abe rose to the occasion, "Oh, yes, the noted poet."

"Are you familiar with my work, Mr. President?"

"To some extent. … *'This fresh young world I see, / With heroes, cities, legends of her own …'* … That's one of yours, isn't it." Turning to his son, he said, "Thomas, why didn't you tell us your lady-friend was a poet on the order of a Whittier, or a Christina Rossetti, or either of the Brownings?" Both Thomas and Emma blushed.

Florence tried to change the subject to something less embarrassing to the two young people when a red-haired young man rushed into the restaurant. He wore a bellboy's uniform from the Fifth Avenue Hotel, where Florence was staying. He was out of breath, having ridden his bicycle furiously from the hotel on Madison Square. He approached the table where the five were sitting and said, with a broad Irish brogue, "Miss Nightingale. An urgent telegram has arrived for you at the hotel. Here it is."

She opened the envelope and read the telegram.

She gave the boy a silver dollar and thanked him, saying that she'll be at the hotel shortly to pack her cases, check out and take the next train to Washington.

Looking at her shocked luncheon companions, she said. "The telegram is from the First Lady. The President was shot. She wants me to come and nurse him. Reading between the lines, I assume she wants me to keep his imbecile doctors from completing the job the assassin began. ... Abe and Mary, please reply to Mrs. Garfield saying I'll be in Washington as soon as I can get on a train. ... Emma, please contact the committees in the various cities to reschedule my lectures but ensuring they know I plan to keep every commitment once I'm free to do so. You have the details in your folder at your home. ... Thomas, please escort me in your carriage to a railway station to see when the next available train would be to Washington. You can bring Emma home on the way."

As the three rushed out, Mary Lincoln said to her husband, "I think we've just seen the same Florence Nightingale who ran roughshod over the generals and the doctors in the Crimea."

Two days later, in Washington, a woman with a commanding air stormed into the President's sickroom in the White House and announced to his doctors, "Gentlemen, please stop poking my patient's wound with your filthy hands! My name is Nightingale, Florence Nightingale. You can call me 'Miss Nightingale', thank you. Mrs. Garfield has hired me to take charge of the hygienic discipline of her husband's sickroom and to keep you from completing the job which Mr. Guiteau began. Wash your hands and please use plenty of soap. On your way out, someone please open a window to let some fresh air in. And this room is now out-of-bounds for smoking. As they say in Italy, 'Capisce?'"

"Capisce, I think," one doctor meekly mumbled.

21. Have a "heap big" good day.

Near Flagstaff in the Protectorates, April 1886

The tall, dark-haired man in a khaki uniform remained on his horse as he replied to the man in the driver's seat of the first of the small group of three wagons.

"How!" he began, replying to the man in the same terms in which the stranger addressed him.

"Now that that's over with, can I suggest we speak in the Queen's English, rather than as if we were cast members of Buffalo Bill's Wild West Show?

"My name is *Lieutenant William Bearclaw* of the Protectorates Militia. As you seemed to surmise, I am in fact what you would call an 'Injun', Cherokee to be exact. My men and I are patrolling this area as part of a joint operation involving troops from the Union, Deseret, and the Protectorates. The Confederate army is busy enough guarding the Louisiana and Arkansas borders to station any men here in the Protectorates.

"My 'heap big chief', as you so colourfully put it, is *Colonel Henry Van Rensselaer* of the United States Army. He's at Fort Hamlin, twenty miles away, so you'll have to settle for me.

"I assume from the fact that your group is made up mostly of women and children, other than yourself, that you are a polygamous family leaving Deseret to settle in Texas. Our task is to ensure that everyone making the trip is doing so voluntarily, and that no one is brought to Texas against their will. From what I know of it, Texas is not a place where I'd want to bring either a woman or a child ... far too dangerous ... far too evil. Even if they hanged that monstrous bastard *Simon Legree* last year for what he did to those girls, there are still plenty of other peculiar men in Texas, and one of the most peculiar of all is that damned Emperor of theirs, pardon my French.

"Anyway, enough of my political opinions. A number of ladies from the Deseret Co-operative Welfare Association will be with you in a few minutes. They will talk to each of your ladies individually, and to each of the children. If you choose not to co-operate with them, you will be escorted back to the Deseret border in handcuffs.

The DCWA ladies will determine who seems to be going to Texas willingly and who is going unwillingly. Those ladies who don't want to go won't be forced to do so. They will be reunited with the families in Deseret. Those with no families in Deseret, or those whose families won't support their being independent, will be assisted to find other, decent ways to support themselves. Smaller children will stay with their mothers. Older children will make their own choices.

"These ladies from the DCWA are magnificent. We call them 'Amanda's Angels' after their founder, *Miss Amanda Kimball*, a wonderful lady. In my opinion she's a North American Florence Nightingale what with the way she's organised the care for these ladies and their children.

"Another thing 'Amanda's Angels' will do for all of you is to give you all a decent meal and arrange for you all to have hot baths, which my nose tells me most of you need after your time on the road.

"After the ladies and children have been sorted out by the DCWA ladies, those of you who want to go to Texas will be guided to the border by three of my men. They know the safe, quick, and easy route to get to the border.

"At the border, at Fort Seward, my men will hand over responsibility for your group to the Union Army chaps stationed there. They'll check your wagons for any items that are contraband. And, of course, you should know that we're not permitting weapons of any sort to enter Texas. Too many brigands from Texas are still raiding communities in the Protectorates (as well as in the Confederacy and Mexico) to enslave innocent people for us to allow arms to get to these bandits. Besides, my brother lost a leg fighting against raiders from Texas. I really don't want to provide them with the weapons to do any more damage to any more people.

"After the inspection, you'll be escorted to the Texas border by an officer of the Union Army and once you cross the border, as Dante once said, 'Abandon all hope, ye who enter here.'

"Well, here's a few of 'Amanda's Angels' and I'll leave you in their capable hands. Have a 'heap big' good day."

22. *Figaro Johnson* and his stock market tip

When he was a little boy, growing up as a "house slave" on a tobacco farm in Virginia, *Figaro Johnson* was always interested in the marks on pieces of paper that many grownups seemed to spend a great deal of time staring at. He was told that some of these marks were letters, which made up words, and that some were numbers. It was against the law at that time to teach slaves how to read, or write, or work with numbers.

Some of the slaves could read, and write, and work with numbers. Most of them hid that skill from the masters. *Old Henry*, the butler, he could do all that. *Figaro* didn't know where *Old Henry* learned it, but he did. *Old Henry* taught *Figaro* what the little squiggles on the paper meant, the sounds of the letters and the values of the numbers. *Old Henry* also taught *Figaro* the art of butlering. *Old Henry* didn't have a son of his own, and *Figaro*'s parents died in an accident with a horse when *Figaro* was small, so *Old Henry* became sort of a father to *Figaro*.

Figaro learned quickly. By the time he was ten, he was reading the newspapers from Richmond and Charlottesville, and he was able to do complicated figuring with numbers. He was also becoming a competent assistant butler to *Old Henry,* setting tables for fancy dinners, pouring wine, carving meat, pouring coffee, helping *Old Henry* manage the house's large wine cellar, and speaking to the masters' fancy guests with the most elegant Tidewater accent imaginable, an accent almost British in its elegance. Many of the guests to the house gave him increasingly large tips for his service, which *Figaro* chose to save.

Figaro, as it turns out, was becoming a self-taught expert on money. He was an avid reader of the financial sections of the newspapers. He knew which businesses were doing well and which were doing poorly. He was interested in the changing circumstances of the financial world.

Young Mr. Charles, who was only about two years older than *Figaro*, was also aware of Figaro's interest in finances. *Young Mr. Charles* was the master's oldest son. He encouraged the young slave in his studies. He organised an account for *Figaro* at the local bank, something that wasn't legal for a slave to possess. On trips to Richmond, he bought stocks and shares, some for *Figaro* with *Figaro*'s money, some for himself (at *Figaro*'s advice) with his own.

When *Young Mr. Charles* went off as a student to Princeton in 1857, he asked his father to assign the sixteen-year-old *Figaro* as his valet (a customary practice for slaveholding students going north to Princeton). In addition to the valet's duties, *Figaro* read widely from *Young Mr. Charles*'s books, and ran an unofficial investment business for *Young Mr. Charles*'s friends. When *Young Mr. Charles* returned to Virginia with his degree in 1861, both he and *Figaro* had made a small fortune from keeping the friends of *Young Mr. Charles* financially solvent.

By that time, *Young Mr. Charles* found that his father (known by the slaves as *Old Mr. Charles*) was increasingly ill and was, in fact, dying. Neither *Young Mr. Charles* nor his younger brother, *Ben* (now a sophomore at William and Mary), had ever showed any interest in farming. The farm was to be sold after *Old Mr. Charles* death with the proceeds being split between *Young Mr. Charles*, *Ben*, and *Old Mr. Charles's* widow.

The family owned two comfortable town houses, one in Richmond and one in Nashville. *Young Mr. Charles* would determine which of these houses he'd inherit and which one would go to *Ben*. *Old Mr. Charles*'s widow would determine with which of her sons she'd live. The farm slaves would be sold. *Young Mr. Charles* would determine which of the house slaves would go to Nashville, which would go to Richmond, which would be freed, and which would be sold.

The brothers easily determined that *Young Mr. Charles* preferred Nashville and *Ben* preferred Richmond. (Ben took a year of from his studies.) As their mother had a sister and many friends from her schooldays in Richmond, her choice was also easy. Neither brother wanted a large number of house slaves, but *Figaro* and (at *Figaro*'s urging) the now-blind *Old Henry* were among *Young Mr. Charles*'s choices.

After the funeral, the reading of the will, and the selling up of the property, *Young Mr. Charles*, *Figaro*, *Old Henry*, and a small handful of house slaves were off to Nashville. Once they crossed the Tennessee state line, *Young Mr.*

Charles simply became known as *Mr. Charles*. No one said anything about the change. It just happened.

In Nashville, *Mr. Charles* set up a business, called *Charles Claiborne and Associates, Stockbrokers*. It was to advise rich men how to invest their money to become even richer. The "Associates" in the business's name were actually one associate: *Figaro*. "You're worth two or even three associates," *Mr. Charles* told *Figaro*. "You have a head for numbers, and you can make sense out of even the most convoluted annual report or financial statement."

Mr. Charles's contribution to the business was to take his rich friends out to lunch to persuade them to send some business his way. This wasn't merely an exercise in public relations. The conversations in the private gentlemen's clubs he frequented often centred around which prominent businessmen were seen drunk far too often, or noted as hiring far too many incompetent nephews or sons-in-law for key positions in their companies, or spending far too much on their expensive mistresses. ("Is it his own money, or company money? That's what I'd like to know," was a frequent question.) This information on the "non-operational risks" for some companies, coupled with the information that *Figaro* could decipher from the annual reports and financial statements, made the financial advice offered by *Charles Claiborne* and Associates some of the best on either side of the border.

Figaro was technically *Mr. Charles's* butler but. other than supervising the keeping of the household accounts and assisting *Old Henry* in ordering wine for the cellar, his butler's duties were performed by more junior members of the staff.

Even though *Figaro* was now almost as wealthy a man as *Mr. Charles*, he was still a slave. He could have easily bought his freedom, but he wanted *Mr. Charles* to bring up the subject. *Mr. Charles* wanted *Figaro* to bring up the subject. Both were proud, stubborn men.

So it continued for decades. Each of the men married. *Mr. Charles's* wife, *Arabella*, came from the North. *Figaro's* wife, *Betty*, was once a cook in *Mr. Charles's* home and had bought her freedom. Like *Figaro*, *Betty* was also a Catholic, at that time in history a rare occurrence among African-Americans.

Each man had a son. *Charles Claiborne III* went to college at Sewanee when he was old enough. *Florestan Johnson* went to Fisk. (With both he and *Betty* being opera lovers, *Figaro* gave his son an operatic name like his own, thus beginning a family tradition, which continued when *Florestan* named his twin sons *Falstaff* and *Faust*.) The two boys were close friends from their childhood. Both played quarterback for their colleges' football teams. Both hounded their fathers about addressing the issue of *Figaro's* status as a slave. ("The first move is *Figaro's*," said *Mr. Charles* to his son. "The first move is *Mr. Charles's*," said *Figaro* likewise to his son.)

It was July of 1893. *Figaro* was fifty-two. *Mr. Charles* was fifty-four. Their sons had recently received their degrees. The *Nashville American* reported that the last known slave in the Confederacy, an elderly valet in Savannah, had been freed following the death of his owner. At the last count, there were only about seven slaves remaining within the Union, all household servants in cities such as Nashville, Memphis, Richmond, and Baltimore. (The last known slaves other than household servants were freed in the Union in 1877 and in the Confederacy in 1881.) The article posed the question, "Now that the Confederacy is free from slavery, can the Union be far behind?"

While both *Figaro* and *Mr. Charles* had read the article, along with their wives and their sons, they hadn't discussed the article with each other. They were concerned about the future of the *Bank of Southwestern Tennessee*. The Bank was in grave financial difficulties. Many of their depositors had withdrawn all their cash. Shares in the Bank were selling at an all-time low. However, *Mr. Charles* had overheard some plans were in progress to save the Bank. A number of other banks were planning to buy up the Bank's shares. The price of shares would soon go up dramatically once the other banks started buying up the shares. There was money to be made, if *Figaro* and *Mr. Charles* could get their hands on some cash. However, all of their cash was committed to other investments.

Their sons, who were also working for the firm, were in the office one Tuesday afternoon in late July while the discussion was happening. *Charles Claiborne III* (known, according to Southern tradition as *"Trey"*) said to his father, "You could always follow the example of *George Mackenzie.*" *Florestan* started laughing.

"*George Mackenzie?*"

"*George Mackenzie*, of *Mackenzie and Murphy*, the tailors in Baltimore," replied *Trey*.

Figaro contributed, "*Mackenzie and Murphy*, they make fine suits. The last time I was in Baltimore, I bought one of their ..."

Florestan interrupted his father with a quote he'd read on a magazine article: "This here boy's my slave and I'm a'fixin' to set him free. Where do we get our money?" *Trey,* who'd read the same article, doubled over with laughter.

Mr. Charles said, looking at *Figaro*, "This may be an idea. They're still giving out the manumission money. Between my money and yours, that will buy a decent parcel of bank shares. Let's head off to the clerk's office and then let's see how many shares we can buy with the money." Looking at *Florestan*, he said, "It may be an idea for you to let your mother know that her husband is soon to be a free man ... as well as a much richer one."

By the following Monday, the sign in front of the brokerage office read *"Claiborne, Johnson, and Sons, Stockbrokers"*.

When the *Nashville American* reported a few weeks later that final slave to be set free in the Union had, in fact, been liberated, and that the ex-slave was, in fact, one *Figaro*

Johnson of Nashville, formerly a butler but now a stockbroker, the popping of champagne corks was heard in the office, as it was also heard in many places around the continent. Now, for slavery as well as for polygamy, Texas was the last hold-out for either "peculiar institution" on the North American continent.

23. "God bless us every one!" (part 2)

The White House, Washington, Thanksgiving Day, 1893.

One place where champagne was uncorked in 1893 in honour of Figaro Johnson's freedom was the White House, on a number of occasions. One of those occasions was Thanksgiving Dinner.

Robert Lincoln was in the first year of his term, having succeeded Benjamin Harrison earlier in the year. Lincoln was the second presidential son, after John Quincy Adams, to also serve as President. After serving in diplomatic posts in Salt Lake City and Montgomery during the Hayes administration, he spent four years representing the Union in London during the Garfield administration. He returned to his Chicago law practice during the Pats' brief turn in power under Grover Cleveland, before serving as Benjamin Harrison's Vice-President. He defeated Cleveland easily in 1892, with William McKinley as his running mate, returning the Progressives to office.

The President and the First Lady, Mary Eunice Lincoln, along with their eighteen-year-old daughter Jessie, hosted a number of family members and friends at the White House. The President's elder daughter, Mamie, was in Vermont with her husband and small child.

The first of the extended Lincoln family to arrive were Thomas and his ten-year-old son *David*, arriving by train from New York. Thomas Lincoln married Emma Lazarus soon after she met his parents in 1880. They had one child, *David*, born in 1883. In the year of *David*'s birth,

Emma wrote a poem "The New Colossus", in honour of the Statue of Liberty which was in the process of construction. By the time the Statue was completed in 1886, Emma's health was deteriorating and she died in November of 1887.

Abe Lincoln was already in Washington, staying at the Willard. He had been a widower since Mary's death in 1882. It took Abe a long time to adjust to living on his own, but he spent much of his time travelling between the homes of his sons in various locations. Essentially, he carried his grief in a very Victorian manner.

"You won't believe who I ran into at the Willard," said Abe. (Abe always stayed at the Willard when he was in Washington. Not even having a son living in the White House would change that.)

"I'll take a stab at Tommy Meagher," said Robert.

"Yes, *David* and I were talking to Tommy and his wife Elizabeth on the train from New York," said Thomas. "He seems to have thrived in retirement. He's properly become what the French call a *boulevardier*. He's seen almost everywhere in New York. He knows everybody. He's invited to all the right parties. He has opinions on everything, and for the most part, the opinions are highly witty and entertaining."

"And what are the Meaghers doing in Washington?" asked Abe.

"*David* asked Tommy that same question on the train. What did he say, *Dave*?" said Thomas.

"The same reason you're going to Washington," he said, "to have Thanksgiving Dinner at the White House."

"Excellent!" exclaimed Abe.

Thomas and Elizabeth Meagher arrived soon after. While Elizabeth carried herself with the dignified air of those born to wealth, Thomas had the same casual Irish affability that served him well in diplomatic posts in Salt Lake City and Montgomery during those critical years when the three nations were institutionally disentangling themselves with each other while committed to continuing friendly relations. (It was Meagher who first coined the term "the velvet divorce" for this process.) This was followed by eight years as Seward's successor as Secretary of State in the Lee and Blaine administrations. A return to journalism followed, along with writing a few popular novels.

He greeted each of the assembled Lincolns with a formal flourish. "Mr. President, ... Madame First Lady, ... Miss Jessie, ... Mr. President again, ... Maestro Tomasso, ... Young Mr. David, ... and where is his Reverence the Bishop?"

"Here I am. Our train from St. Augustine was late." A young man, at least young-looking for a bishop, came into the room with two middle-aged men, a short clergyman leaning on a walking stick and a slim, African-American man with a Van Dyke beard.

"Hello, Tommy, I haven't seen you since Salt Lake City," said the black man.

"Alex, my old partner in crime, or should that be diplomacy?" said the Irishman. Both laughed.

"I see Secretary Meagher remembers my friend Dr. Darnes," said the bishop.

Meagher flamboyantly kissed the bishop's ring, shook hands with the other cleric, who spoke with an English accent, and gave the black man a bear hug. "I was so sorry to hear of your brother's passing earlier this year."

"Yes, it was only after he left office as President that Ed felt that he was able to be honest that his father was also my father, but nevertheless, for the eight years until his death in March, we were warmly and openly brothers."

William Lincoln, who was appointed as Bishop of St. Augustine, Florida, earlier in the year at the young age of 43, called out to all, "I should introduce my two guests. Many of you have already met *Father Tim Cratchit* in England. With thanks to the Oratorian Fathers in Birmingham for releasing him for parish duties, I recently appointed him as priest of the parish I served in Jacksonville for the seven years between my arrival in Florida and becoming bishop. The distinguished medical gentleman is Dr. Alexander Darnes, also of Jacksonville, who was one of only three or four doctors who remained in the city to care for the sick during the Yellow Fever epidemic of '88. As you may have gathered from Alex's conversation with Tommy, Alex is also the brother of the late Confederate President Edmund Kirby-Smith."

Abe Lincoln called out, "Another one of the generation of the 1860s who has departed ... Seward, ... Benjamin, ... Beauregard, ... Davis, ... Hamlin, ... Lee, ... Kirby-Smith. ... Nevertheless, Jim Longstreet lives."

"And Abe Lincoln lives," interjected Meagher to the loud cheers of the Lincolns and their guests.

"And Tommy Meagher lives," replied Abe to the laughter and applause of all.

"Dinner is served," said a butler.

As the Lincolns and their guests gathered in the dining room, Robert Lincoln announced "As we begin, I assume that Bishop William will offer grace."

"No, I was talking with our nephew *David* and he's learning some Hebrew graces in preparation for his Bar Mitzvah. I propose that David offers our thanks today.

David blushed and put on his yarmulke, as did his father, who converted to Judaism before his wedding. He said, "It's still a few years before my Bar Mitzvah, but I'm learning some basic Hebrew prayers." He picked up a roll, held it up, and said *"Baruch attah, Adonai, Elohenu, melech haolam. Hamotzi lechem min haaretz. ...* Blessed are you, Lord God, king of the universe. You bring forth bread from the earth."

A halting "Amen" followed from the others at the table, with *David's* father and the two clerics being the first to respond.

David lifted a wineglass and continued, "*Baruch attah, Adonai Elohenu, melech haolam. Boray pe'ri hagofen.* ... Blessed are you, Lord God, king of the universe. You bring forth the fruit of the vine."

A much more confident "Amen" resounded around the table, as *David* and Thomas removed their yarmulkes and the soup was served.

Between the soup and the main course, Robert said, "Before the end of the meal, I'd like to invite any of our guests who wish to do so, to offer a toast."

Dr. Darnes stood and said, "Thank you, Mr. President. I would like to offer a toast to a man who represents a great hope both to this nation and to the nation to our immediate South. Earlier this year, in the city of Nashville, a slave named *Figaro Johnson* was freed. As things turned out, *Mr. Johnson* was the last person to be held as a slave in either the Union or the Confederacy. As a person who was born a slave myself, I know how precious a thing freedom is. Let the freeing of Mr. Johnson be seen by all as a sign of a new era of hope. Let us all stand. Ladies and gentlemen, Let us all toast *Figaro Johnson*."

"To *Figaro Johnson*." All drained their glasses of champagne.

After a moment's silence, Abe Lincoln looked around and said, "And the task is not yet complete. The curse of slavery and the curse of polygamy are still realities in Texas. The Union, the Confederacy, Deseret, Texas, and the Protectorates are still five different societies. I won't see the day myself, but let us all work, pray, and hope for the day when slavery on this continent is no more ... even in Texas. Let us all work, pray, and hope for the day when polygamy on this continent is no more ... even in Texas. Let us all work, pray, and hope for the day when, once again, there is only one great republic occupying the land from the Atlantic to the Pacific, from the Great Lakes to the Rio Grande."

All began to applaud, but Abe held up his hands and said, "Let me finish." He brought two venerable-looking bottles from out of a satchel and put them on the table. "These two bottles of excellent French cognac were given to Mary and myself by the late Cardinal Newman. (He was still Father Newman at the time.) There were six bottles, but the others were consumed by us, to our great satisfaction I must add. Of these remaining two bottles, I propose we drink one bottle after dinner this evening, in honour of *Figaro Johnson*, Alex Darnes, and all who were once slaves and are now free. The other bottle I place in the safe-keeping of the President." He gave the bottle to Robert.

He continued, "This bottle shall be consumed at my graveside in Springfield, by all those living who are now around this table, when three things have taken place. The first will be that slavery on this continent is no more ... even in Texas. The second will be that polygamy on this continent will be no more ... even in Texas. The third will be that the Union, the Confederacy, Deseret, the

Protectorates, and even poor old Texas will once again be a single nation."

"And what if the cognac's gone sour by that time?" asked Tommy Meagher.

"Well, then it will be one hell of an expensive salad dressing," replied Thomas Lincoln. All laughed.

"And worth every cent of it," added Abe.

After a few moments of awkward silence, *Father Cratchit* stood and added, "I, too would like to offer a toast. It was a toast I frequently gave at family celebrations as a child, and which I also often offered in our community of priests in England. I wish to offer it now, both for all of us around this table, and for this land so fraught with danger and so brimming with hope. As a man of the Old World, I offer this toast for the New. Let us stand. Ladies and gentlemen, God bless us, every one."

"God bless us, every one," all replied.

24. "Which one?"

The 1895 Confederate election proved to be a watershed. Georgia Congressman Hoke Smith was elected as the youngest president in the Confederacy's history, at the age of 40. At the time of secession, he was a little boy of five. A strong Progressive, he was to serve slightly more than six five-year terms as President from his initial election until he retired at the time of Reunion in 1926. For most of Hoke Smith's time as President in Montgomery, his *bete noire* was his fellow Georgian Tom Watson, leader of the Populist Party of the Confederacy, a politician whose almost pathological racism, antisemitism, and anti-Catholicism would have struck a responsive chord among many southern – and, indeed, northern - voters in the 1850s, but who was seen as an anachronism in his own day.

For almost twenty years, from the election of Hoke Smith in 1895 until the death of "Young Joseph" in 1914, it was a running joke in Washington that an aide would rush into the President's office with an urgent message from "President Smith", to which the President would reply "Which one?" (A third "President Smith", a former Governor of New York, would later appear in Washington just before Reunion, but this would be ten years after the death of "Young Joseph".)

In Texas, during the reigns of *Alois II* and *Ignaz II* in the 1890s, the small but steady stream of polygamists moving to Texas to flee the marriage reforms being enacted in Deseret led to legislation generally allowing all white males in Texas, regardless of their religious affiliation, to practice polygamy. Increasingly, a number of non-Mormon Texan men, particularly wealthy and politically well-connected slaveowners, decided they wanted to practice polygamy, even if they didn't share a theology that allowed for the practice. By the late 1890s, the majority of Texan polygamists were non-Mormons. While most churches in Texas resisted pressure from the government to allow their members to practice polygamy, the Texas Baptist Convention split over the issue of polygamy with the larger faction voting to allow their pastors to perform polygamous marriages.

In Washington, Robert Lincoln was succeeded as President after the 1896 election by his Vice-President, William McKinley. McKinley's election was the first of many in which the unsuccessful candidate for the Populists was William Jennings Bryan.

One of McKinley's first official tasks as President was to attend the state funeral of Abraham Lincoln, who died at the age of 88, a few days after McKinley succeeded Robert. (According to some wits, Lincoln's legendary kindness and courtesy even extended to his time of death, occurring when Robert could participate in the funeral as Abe's son, not as the serving President; and also occurring at a time when many of the dignitaries wishing to attend the state funeral were already in Washington for the inauguration.) In addition to Abe's sons and grandson, the pallbearers included Tommy Meagher, "Young Joseph", James Longstreet, and Hoke Smith.

Two other mourners, defying the nineteenth-century custom that women of the upper and middle classes did not attend funerals, were Florence Nightingale (already in America on another one of her frequent lecture tours) and a daughter of Queen Victoria (already in America in connection with an artistic exhibition), representing her mother. Well-placed gossips on both sides of the Atlantic had linked Miss Nightingale romantically with Abe Lincoln and had linked the Marchioness romantically with each of Abe's sons at various times. All of these rumours were true. (In the case of William, this was before his ordination as a priest, an event which inspired the Marchioness to confide to a friend "What a waste!" In the case of Thomas, it was well before he met Emma Lazarus. In the case of Abe, it was well after Mary's death, and was essentially a matter of a lonely widower and a lonely spinster finding joy in each other's company.) The fact that this gossip did not find its way into print during the lifetimes of any of those directly involved was a tribute to the discretion of the journalistic community at the time.

A few months after his father's funeral, Robert Lincoln accepted an appointment as Provost of Trinity College, Dublin. He sailed for Ireland with his family in the summer and remained in Ireland until he retired from academic life after the end of the Great War. Based in Dublin, he visited Britain frequently and engaged in useful unofficial diplomacy on behalf of the Union and the other nations of North America.

Like his fellow presidential son who also served as President, John Quincy Adams, Robert was one of a select group of ex-presidents whose post-presidential career was as distinguished as his time in the White House. Rumours among diplomatic sources in Britain and Ireland have long maintained that King George V's decision to commute the death sentences of the leaders of the 1916 Easter Rising in Dublin to five years' imprisonment was largely the result of a golf course conversation between the King and the former President.

It was in the 1890s that the system of Protectorates, initially set up to develop mostly self-governing homelands for Native Americans under the joint auspices of the Union, the Confederacy, and Deseret, expanded to include areas outside the North American continent. Following the end of the Spanish-American War in 1898, which the Union and the Confederacy fought against Spain (and in which Deseret chose to remain neutral), a number of Spanish overseas possessions (Cuba, Puerto Rico, Guam, and the Philippines) passed into the joint control of the Union and Confederacy.

The Joint Department of Protectorates was given asked to take over responsibility for these areas. This was alongside the Native American areas (which were divided into the three separate Protectorates of Oklahoma, New Mexico, and Arizona) along with the Hawaiian Islands and the eastern islands of the Samoan group, which were acquired in the late 19th century by various treaties and, at least in the case of Hawaii, a large amount of chicanery.

(Shortly before the beginning of the Great War, Denmark sold its Caribbean possessions in the Virgin Islands to the Joint Department of Protectorates to prevent them falling into German hands.)

McKinley was succeeded after the 1900 election by Theodore Roosevelt, the young Governor of New York and a swashbuckling cavalry officer from the war with Spain. Roosevelt was a popular President and was the first inhabitant of the White House since Andrew Jackson to be elected to a second term. (Only two of Roosevelt's successors, Woodrow Wilson and Al Smith, were elected to second terms.)

One reason for Roosevelt's popularity was his administration's policies regarding the regulation of banks, corporations, and other businesses. Many economists, both American and international, credit the regulatory reforms put in place by the Roosevelt administration and, later, by the Wilson and Smith administrations with establishing a sense of economic stability which enabled the economy to withstand the pressures of the 1929 Wall Street panic so that a three-year-long national recession did not spiral out into a potentially decade-long global depression.

Nevertheless, the many achievements (economic and otherwise) of the Roosevelt administration were nearly destroyed before they had a chance to begin. An attempt by a group of anarchists to assassinate Roosevelt at an International Exposition in Buffalo in 1901 was foiled as a result of some clever espionage work. *Florestan Johnson,*

son of the noted Nashville stockbroker and a partner in the family firm, was looking for a more exciting life than the world of finance. He joined the Army, was accepted into officer training, and was assigned to the Intelligence Corps. One of his earliest assignments was to penetrate an anarchist cell. He uncovered a plot on the life of the President, which led to a series of arrests and trials, and to *Johnson* becoming an overnight sensation in the popular press (as well as receiving a series of rapid promotions in rank).

One of those whose imaginations were stirred by *Johnson*'s exploits was *David Lincoln*, then a freshman at Lafayette College. *Dave* was uncertain as to whether his future involved politics and law (like his grandfather and uncle), music (like his father), literature (like his mother), or perhaps even the rabbinate (in some ways, following in the footsteps of his uncle, the bishop). The one certainty in his life was his sporting prowess. Even as a freshman, he was the Leopards' starting quarterback and distinguished himself in the annual match against Lehigh.

However, reading of *Florestan Johnson*'s exploits, *Dave* considered whether a military career, perhaps in intelligence, was his future. As it turned out, *Dave Lincoln* not only became a brilliant intelligence officer but, following the Great War, succeeded *Florestan Johnson* as the head of Army Intelligence.

In the mid-1930's, *Dave* and his team were responsible for a number of major intelligence breakthroughs. They discovered the plans for Italy's invasion of Ethiopia and were able to organise covert assistance for the Ethiopians (involving units of the United States Marines, the Royal Marines, and the French Foreign Legion) to defeat the invasion, leading to riots in many Italian cities and Mussolini's overthrow. At roughly the same time, they uncovered plans for a coup in Spain, and shared the information with the Spanish government, leading to the exile of the main conspirator, General Franco.

By 1941, *Dave* and the team had the information of the plans by the Japanese forces to attack Pearl Harbor on the 7th of December. The Japanese planes were intercepted well before they were anywhere near Honolulu. A potentially long Pacific War became a short one. By this time, *Florestan Johnson*'s son *Falstaff* was *Dave Lincoln*'s assistant, and succeeded him after his retirement at the end of the Pacific War. (*Falstaff Johnson* was head of US Army Intelligence during the early stages of that lengthy conflict in South Africa when American, British, and Commonweath forces assisted the multiracial government of South Africa against white supremacist rebels. During this time, *Johnson* worked closely with the head of MI6's South African operations, the Royal Navy's *Commander Bond, ... James Bond.*)

But all this is getting far ahead of ourselves, and the period of the Roosevelt administration.

At the end of Roosevelt's second term, the Progressives nominated Roosevelt's Vice-President Robert LaFollette as their presidential candidate for the 1908 presidential election, while the Pops nominated William Jennings Bryan for the fourth time in a row, and the Pats nominated an Ohio judge named William Howard Taft, a genial, heavy-set Santa Claus of a man.

Taft's size and bearing assisted him in his campaign. Around the English-speaking world, it was the Edwardian era, a time in which excess was embraced and austerity was avoided. If anyone could have been regarded as an American Edwardian, it was Taft, who easily defeated his austere opponents, the teetotal Bryan and the vegetarian LaFollette, in the 1908 election.

By 1912, the Progressives had regrouped and nominated the Governor of New Jersey (and the former president of Princeton University) Woodrow Wilson as President. The Virginia-born Wilson easily defeated Taft and Bryan in the election, and began to re-emphasise the economic policies promoted by Roosevelt.

25. *"Ho fatto a modo mio…."*

In the mid-1890s, Texas was the only place in the western world to practice either slavery or polygamy. This continued until the end of the Great War. As a result, a sometimes ghoulish fascination developed with Texas in the popular imaginations of Europeans. This fascination was particularly reflected in three distinctly different cultural works.

W.S. Gilbert and Sir Arthur Sullivan: *The Earl of El Paso (1898)*

The Earl of El Paso (or "The Reluctant Polygamist") was Gilbert and Sullivan's final collaboration, produced after their mediocre efforts ***Utopia Limited (1893)*** and ***The Grand Duke (1896)***. It was a return to the sparkling wit of their earlier successes. Lord Rupert Trelawney-Macintosh, recently installed as the Earl of Downmarket, suddenly left his estates and travelled incognito to North America to escape the annoying attentions of Amaryllis Blimpington, whose wealth as the heiress to a wealthy confectionary manufacturer was her only redeeming quality in Rupert's eyes.

Rupert knew that his late father had spent some of his youthful years in Texas, sowing wild oats and owning a cattle ranch which, Rupert was told, would be part of his inheritance. Rupert, being short of actual money (even if he had the titles to an Irish earldom, a Yorkshire viscountcy, two Cornish baronetcies, and two Scottish lairdships), knew that a profitable Texan cattle ranch would be useful to keeping himself in the style in which he wished to become accustomed. However, Rupert was followed (unbeknownst to him) by Amaryllis Blimpington, accompanied by her Jamaican lady's maid Matilda Maddingley.

The story continued in typical Gilbertian fashion. At Downmarket Ranch in Texas, Rupert met his two half-brothers, with each of the three having a different mother. One of the half-brothers, Wayne Westward, was a polygamous slaveowner, who felt great reluctance to participate in either "peculiar institution", but did so because he was told it was his "duty". Rupert's other half-brother, Dwayne Dalton, was Wayne's slave and ostensible "valet", although his real role was to act (*a la Figaro Johnson*) as Wayne's financial advisor. The three half-brothers realised their family relationship when Rupert noticed that each of the others had the distinctive family birthmark (shaped like a cricket bat) on the back of their left knees. (Well, it *is* Gilbert and Sullivan, after all.)

Happy endings abound, along with four patter songs, three love duets, and an enthusiastic Caribbean dance (taught by Matilda to the men's and ladies' choruses) as the first act *finale*. Amaryllis and Matilda each fall madly (and comically) in love with one of Rupert's half-brothers, with the affections being happily returned. Rupert similarly develops a relationship with Esther Easterbrook, one of Wayne's many *fiancees ("whom he reckons up by dozens"),* with each of whom Wayne resided in an uncomfortable and nervous celibacy. The shrewd investments made by the enslaved financial wizard result in the three half-brothers being fabulously wealthy. Each of the slaves and each of the plural wives on the ranch were freed.

A typically Gilbertian triple wedding followed (Rupert and Esther, Wayne and Amaryllis, Dwayne and Matilda), with Rupert giving his half-brothers a baronetcy and a lairdship each as a wedding present. A rousing final chorus (and a reprise of the Caribbean dance) are all that remains before the final curtain calls.

Giacomo Puccini: *Lionel e Jolene* (1908)

Puccini wrote **Lionel e Jolene** four years after **Madama Butterfly** *(1904)*. Particularly compared with the comedy of Gilbert and Sullivan's **The Earl of El Paso,** this was a markedly tragic work.

The opera begins by introducing Lionel, a slave on a Texas cattle ranch who was hopelessly (and, he believed, unrequitedly) in love with Jolene, engaged to be one of the polygamous wives of Orrin Peterson, the owner of the ranch. Lionel expresses his fantasy of running away to sea in his aria **"Nella marina, puoi navigare I sette mari...."** *("In the navy, you can sail the seven seas....")* In the years following, until the Great War, humming or whistling the tune to **"Nella marina"** became a secret signal used among resistance groups in Texas to help opponents of the regime to identify each other.

Unknown to Lionel, Jolene returned his affections and agonised over her love for Lionel and her family's expectation that she marry the wealthy Orrin, expressed in her aria *"A volte è difficile una donna…."* *("You know it's hard to be a woman….")* The chorus of Orrin's many wives reply to Jolene's dilemma with an unconcerned *"Fai il tuo uomo…."* *("Stand by your man….")*

The role of Orrin has long been considered one of the "meatiest" villians' parts in all opera, both musically and dramatically. He has three great dramatic arias:

Early in the production, Orrin observes Lionel's effortless charisma, a charisma which impels women of all races to desire him and men of all races to respect him, a quality which Orrin knew he lacked and which he fatally craved. Orrin mocked Lionel behind his back in the aria *"Uomo macho…."* *("Macho man….")*

As Lionel developed his plan to murder both Lionel and Jolene in cold blood, he admitted the evil of his inner nature to the audience, not apologetically but boastfully, in the aria *"Sono cattivo. Sono cattivo. Sai che sono cattivo…."* *("I'm bad. I'm bad. You know that I'm bad….")*

At the conclusion of the opera, as the chorus of slaves and plural wives tie Orrin up with stout ropes and prepare to hurl him into the Rio Grande, he sings, with defiance *"Ho fatto a modo mio…."* *("I did it my way….")*

Agatha Christie: *Murder on the Orient Express* (1934)

Fictional murders similar to the murder committed by Orrin in ***Lionel e Jolene*** provided the backstory to Agatha Christie's Murder on the Orient Express, written eight years after the reunification of the United States, but at a time when Europeans were still fascinated by the combination of slavery, polygamy, and rampant corruption found in the pre-war Texan Empire.

The victim of the murder in the title was a mysterious Italian financier named Cassetti, an associate of Mussolini. The great Belgian detective Hercule Poirot, travelling on the same train, was called in by the railway to investigate.

Using his "little grey cells", Poirot discovers that Cassetti was, in fact, Samuel Ratchett, an American who was on the run in Europe since the Great War. Prior to the war, as the slaveholding and polygamous owner of a large Texas cattle ranch, he murdered of his wives and his slaves in cold blood. After the defeat of Texas in the war, he fled to Europe to escape justice, eventually settling in Italy. Family members of Racthett's victims discovered his new identity as Cassetti and, in the hope of taking their revenge, took jobs as servants of Cassetti/Ratchett in the hope of avenging the deaths of his victims, which they did.

Poirot's strict moral compass determines that it would be unjust for the servants to face imprisonment or execution for ridding the world of the monster Ratchett, and so he determined to inform the authorities that the murder was committed by an unknown assailant, who had (in all probability) left the train immediately after killing Cassetti.

26. "Welcome to Texas, gentlemen. We've gone home."

By the time the Great War broke out in 1914, it was clear that Texas would side with the Central Powers of Germany, Austria, and Turkey. The fact that members of the Hapsburg dynasty had been on the Texan throne since the Empire was established in 1867 provided a strong link between Texas and Austria. Military planners in Berlin, Vienna, and Constantinople saw a supply of Texan beef and Texan petroleum as an essential part of the war effort of the Central Powers. Members of the Texas elite saw war as an opportunity to expand the borders of Texas, casting an eye on the Protectorates to the north and the west, and on Louisiana and Arkansas to the east.

In the other nations of North America, particularly within the Union, there were citizens of German background who wanted either to side with the Kaiser's regime or (at least) to remain neutral. However, the majority of citizens in the Union, the Confederacy, Deseret, and the Protectorates wanted to support Britain and France or, at the very least, to prevent an Texan land grab.

With the decision of Texas to side with the Central Powers, taken merely days after the outbreak of war, an agreement was reached by the governments in Washington, Montgomery, and Salt Lake City that:

1. Any invasion of either the Protectorates or the Confederacy by forces of the Empire of Texas

would be seen as an attack on all the democracies of North America.
2. The Union, the Confederacy, and Deseret will not permit Texan beef or Texan petroleum to be used in the war efforts of Germany, Austria, or Turkey.
3. In the event of war with Texas, the joint goals of the Union, the Confederacy, and Deseret would include the permanent abolition both of slavery and of polygamy in Texas.

Upon the publication of these terms, the government of Texas declared war on the Union, the Confederacy, and Deseret, with the German, Austria, and Turkish governments soon following suit. With the majority of the Confederate Army being concentrated in Arkansas and Louisiana on the Texas border, and with the majority of the Union and Deseret forces similarly located in the Protectorates near the border, the possibilities of an actual war on the North American continent was closer than it was at any time since the 1840s.

Germany, Austria, and Turkey offered troops to assist Texas. While the Austrian forces were largely a token force of ceremonial guards for the Emperor, they freed up a few Texas soldiers for border patrol. The more professional German and Turkish soldiers were assigned to guard the major Gulf Coast ports of Houston and Galveston.

Similarly, other Allied nations also provided small detachments of troops. As forces from the Union, the Confederacy, Deseret, and the Protectorates were already encircling Texas from the east, the north, and the west, the overseas forces were concentrated in northern Mexico, along the Rio Grande, to prevent Texan forces from crossing into Mexico, which was experiencing its own civil war at the time. Forces from France, Britain, and some British dominions (Canada, Australia, and New Zealand) were involved, with Scottish and Irish regiments being particularly prominent in the British forces.

Allied intelligence, as co-ordinated by *Colonel Florestan Johnson* and *Captain David Lincoln* of Union Army intelligence gave a clear picture of low morale in Texas, with high levels of resentment, both among the general population and within the Army, toward the Emperor, and toward the handful of privileged Texans (mostly slaveowners and polygamists) who still supported the Empire. The determination was that, any Allied force entering Texas needed to clearly conduct themselves as liberators, rather than invaders. If they did so, they would be welcomed by the majority of Texans.

The 25th of April, 1915, was chosen as the day for the liberation of Texas. Troops from the Confederacy were to cross the borders from Louisiana and Arkansas. Forces from the Union, the Protectorates, and Deseret would enter from the Protectorates. French, British, Canadian, Australian, and New Zealand regiments would cross the Rio Grande. Units of the United States Marines, the French Foreign Legion, and a few Highland regiments would land from the Gulf, avoiding the areas held by well-disciplined German and Turkish forces in preference to those guarded by Texan conscripts. In terms of the Germans in Houston and the Turks in Galveston, sieges would be far less costly than pitched battles.

As Major-General John Monash led his Australian forces landing at Brownsville, little did he know that the 25th of April would become the date of an annual observance in both Australia and New Zealand to honour war veterans, ANZAC Day (from "Australian and New Zealand Army Corps"). As they approached a Texan trench, they saw a white flag and a large wooden board with writing on it. Monash went up to the board, read the notice, and called his officers together, "Gentlemen our former enemies have left us this message: 'To the Allied forces entering Browsville, good morning, bon jour, and g'day. Welcome to Texas, gentlemen. We've gone home. Signed, the (former) Army of the (former) Empire of Texas.' Form the units! We're marching into Brownsville as liberators. Lieutenant Kelly, please ensure that that this sign is brought back to Australia. Forward, March!" (To this day, the sign is on display in the Australian War Memorial in Canberra.)

As the Australians made their way around and past the poorly-dug Texan trenches, they started to see and hear crowds of people, cheering. Male and female, young and old, of all races: all cheering their liberators. Some musicians were standing in a group, holding their instruments. Their leader called out, "Where are you boys from?"

"Australia!"

The musicians began to play an Australian song. It was a jolly song, about a jolly swagman, who (despite his jollity) nevertheless committed suicide to avoid arrest. The Australians cheered the Texan band.

This scene was repeated around Texas. New Zealand, Canadian, British, French, Union, Confederate, Protectorates, and Deseret soldiers were all treated as liberators by cheering crowds, with the only real resistance being the occasional sniper. Casualties in the Texas Campaign were remarkably low in the context of the bloodbath that marked the Great War in Europe.

In El Paso, the Pennsylvania-born journalist, Richard Harding Davis, accompanying a French regiment, wrote that "their commander, Lt. Colonel Alfred Dreyfus, once a prisoner on Devil's Island, is now the Liberator of El Paso". The title stuck.

In Austin, Maximillian III, realising that his reign was over, dictated a declaration of surrender on 10th May:

1. All forces of the Empire of Texas are ordered to immediately cease military operations and to surrender to the nearest Allied officer.

2. All Austrian, German, and Turkish forces in Texas are encouraged to take similar actions, depending on the orders received from their governments.

3. All persons held as slaves in the Empire of Texas are immediately and unconditionally freed, and slavery is permanently abolished.

4. All polygamous marriages contracted by citizens of the Empire of Texas are immediately and permanently dissolved, and polygamy is permanently abolished.

5. The 1867 decree of Maximillian I by which Texas seceded from the Confederate States of America is hereby annulled, and the Confederacy is hereby invited to take control of the civil government of Texas.

6. The Empire – and the office of Emperor – is hereby abolished.

Maximillian telegraphed this declaration to all his commanders, to the other Central Powers, and to the governments in Washington, Montgomery, and Salt Lake City. He then promptly left town. With the approval of his counterparts in the Union and Deseret, Hoke Smith issued a declaration accepting Maximillian's terms of surrender and agreeing to restore the rule of law in Texas.

All Texan forces – at least, those few which hadn't deserted before 25th April – had surrendered within three days of the Emperor's decree, as did the Austrian forces on ceremonial duties in Austin. It took two more weeks before the Turks in Galveston received orders from Constaninople to surrender. The Kaiser's orders took a few more weeks to arrive in Houston.

By the middle of June, 1915, the Texas Campaign of the Great War was over, as was the Empire of Texas. By that time, the Emperor was nowhere in Texas to be seen. He was travelling through Mexico on his way to exile. Many of his supporters were doing likewise, particularly those who were slaveholders or polygamists. Maximillian eventually made his way to Japan, while many of his supporters looked to the Boer regions of southern Africa. Policymakers in Washington, Montgomery, and Salt Lake City didn't object, as long as they didn't try to bring their slaves or plural wives with them.

The old scheme of "Manumission Bonds" and "Monogamy Bonds" was revived to provide assistance to freed slaves and freed plural wives. (In this case, purchasers of bonds got a bit more "bang for their buck", to use a more modern expression, as all the funds were used to assist the freed slaves and plural wives, rather than to pay off the former slaveholders and former polygamists, most of whom were already outside the country and on the run.

French, British, Canadian, and ANZAC troops were already on their way to the Western Front. Major-General Monash would soon lead his troops in the engagements that led to his eventual knighthood (alongside having both a university and a freeway in Melbourne posthumously named after him, as well as having his face featured on the Australian $100 note). Alfred Dreyfus, the "Liberator of El Paso", returned to France as a national hero and a full Colonel, soon to take charge of the artillery defending Paris.

It would be late in 1917 before many troops from the Union, the Confederacy, the Protectorates, or Deseret would see the Western Front. Many were needed in Texas to serve in the roles usually undertaken by civilian police, at least during the interim before democratic institutions were re-established in Texas. And, as Hoke Smith declared, "In returning Texas to democracy, it is far better that we get it right rather than that we do it fast."

As well, Union, Confederate, Deseret, and Protectorates forces were needed to staff prisoner-of-war camps for Austrian, German, and Turkish personnel. A key demand both of the British and the French was that all forces from the Central Powers would not return to Europe until the end of hostilities. They did not want these troops contributing to the war effort in Europe. Thus, POW camps sprung up near a variety of towns, particularly in the East, with one result being that, both for the prisoners and for their guards, their war was effectively over. Conditions in these camps were generally fairly good, as POW camps go. Morale was generally high.

Even with high morale, the POWs were not immune to the Spanish Influenza pandemic. While battlefield casualties in the Texas campaign were remarkably low, the number of deaths from Spanish Influenza in the POW camps was high, both among the prisoners and their guards.

One POW out of many who died of Spanish Influenza was a German corporal named Adolf Hitler, who died in the POW camp near Blairsville, Pennsylvania, on the 1st of October 1918. In civilian life, Hitler was a minor artist, whose mediocre landscapes (not to mention his frighteningly surrealistic nudes) had a few poorly-received public exhibitions in galleries in Vienna and Munich.

In our own day, Hitler's name is really only known to specialised art historians and to the makers of historical documentaries for television. In almost all nations, it has become a *cliché* of television documentaries about the Great War for the closing moments of the program to include a *pastiche* of the works of artists whose death in the war occurred before they achieved their artistic maturity, so as to illustrate the waste of modern warfare. In these moments, the lacklustre landscapes of Hitler are frequently juxtaposed with the poems of Rupert Brooke and the music of Edward Septimus Kelly.

In the camps, about 15% of Turkish prisoners expressed interest in immigration, with a particular interest in Texas. As the Confederacy had accepted responsibility for the civil affairs of Texas, these prisoners were interviewed by Confederate officials. The vast majority of these applicants were accepted, and relocated to Texas after the Armistice. They and their families became the basis for the vibrant Turkish-American community that we now find in Texas and nearby states.

27. "For such a time as this"

Paris, May 1919

On a breezy May morning in Paris in 1919, Hoke Smith entered the hall at the beginning of yet another session of the Parish Peace Conference. The talks had been underway since January, with little hope of anything positive emerging.

While many of the nations represented wished to use the conference to reduce the chances of any future war breaking out, others seemed determined to seek their own interests, regardless of the consequences. In particular, the French and British delegations (along with the delegations of some of the British dominions) were determined to humiliate Germany, and to grab some German territory in the bargain.

The delegations from North America were trying their best. The Canadians took as independent a stance as the British would allow. The Union's delegation was led by the increasingly frail and ill Woodrow Wilson, nearing the end of his second term as President. The young Secretary of State of Deseret, Elbert Thomas was his country's sole representative. The Oklahoma legislator Will Rogers was sent by the Protectorates, but not seated by the conference. (Thomas offered Rogers a place at the conference as an advisor to the Deseret delegation. An unlikely friendship developed between the professorial Thomas and the former rodeo performer and vaudevillian Rogers.) Particularly given Wilson's poor health, Smith served as the de facto leader of the North Americans.

This morning, Hoke Smith was scheduled to speak. The past few weeks had been frustrating. The British Prime Minister David Lloyd George, the French Prime Minister Georges Clemenceau, and their Australian counterpart William ("Billy") Hughes were redoubling their efforts to bring Germany to its knees in the conference room.

At the appointed time, the chairman introduced Smith to speak. He saw hostile glares on the faces on Lloyd George, Clemenceau, and Hughes, but he was encouraged by the expectant look on the faces of Wilson, Thomas, and Rogers. His aide, the young small-town lawyer from Alabama, *Atticus Finch* (currently serving as a Captain in the Confederate Army) whispered "Knock 'em dead, Mr. President," as he stood to approach the podium.

"Mr. Chairman, honoured colleagues, … I stand here as a man of the New World addressing the nations and civilizations of the Old World with the greatest respect and reverence. It is my privilege to speak the language of Shakespeare, Austen, and Dickens, the language of the Book of Common Prayer and the King James Bible. I speak this noble tongue with joy and with gratitude. To those who speak the languages of Victor Hugo, of Dante, of Homer, and other great figures of our world culture, I also show my respect.

"Our continent has experienced the recent conflict as has yours. Granted, far less blood was spilt on the soil of

Texas than on that of Flanders, but the tears of mothers, wives, and fiancees were no less bitter.

"The people of North America are grateful to the gallant men of Europe and Australasia for their assistance in removing the curse of slavery and the curse of polygamy from our continent. There are areas of Texan cemeteries that will be forever Queensland, forever Normandy, forever Wales.

"The governments of the Confederacy, the Union, Deseret, and (looking squarely at Rogers) the Protectorates are as one in our desire for peace and unity. We celebrate the end of slavery. We celebrate the end of polygamy. We celebrate the fact that former slaves and former plural wives are now citizens with full legal, social, and economic rights, whether they live in Pittsburgh, … Jacksonville, … Provo, … Tulsa, … or San Antonio. We seek to put before our people at the earlier possible occasion a proposal to bring our separated nations together, so that from the Atlantic to the Pacific, and from the Great Lakes to the Rio Grande, there will be only one single great democracy.

"But, as well, we are also one in our determination not to humiliate Texas in any respect.

"And, courteously but firmly, we make the same requests to you (or, as we say in the Confederacy, to y'all). … Do not humiliate Turkey. … Do not humiliate Austria. … Do not humiliate Germany.

"There are many proud and creative nations of people – around the world - who deserve the opportunity to determine their own futures: … Armenians and Koreans, … Poles and Finns, … Czechs and Slovaks, … Jews and Arabs, … Irish and Indians, …" *(At the mention of "Irish and Indians", Lloyd George winced.)* "… Cherokees and Zulus, … Choctaws and Xhosas, … Maoris and Aborigines." (*Hughes winced.*) "We have no moral right to stand in their way.

"Back in 1861, a great statesman named Abraham Lincoln was faced with a choice, a choice between war and peace. Lincoln chose peace. Even though his nation became a bit smaller at the time as a result of that 'Velvet Divorce', the nation that he once governed is now stronger than ever. Mr. Lincoln's Union, along with the Confederacy, Texas, Deseret, and the Protectorates, is now on the verge of a new unity."

Looking at the Australian Prime Minister, Smith said, "Be a Lincoln, Mr. Hughes."

Switching to French, he said "Sois un Lincoln, Monsieur Clemenceau."

And, in Welsh, "Bod yn Lincoln, Mr. Lloyd George."

As Smith began to make for his seat, the hall erupted into applause. The smaller delegations such as the Greeks seemed particularly enthusiastic. The applause developed into a standing ovation. Rogers and Thomas caught the eye of *Captain Finch* and the three began to sing "Dixie". Those who knew the song joined in, while others hummed and clapped in time. By the final "Away, away, away down South in Dixie," even those whose English was non-existent had joined in singing.

Smith saw David Lloyd George scribbling on a piece of paper and leaving a note at Smith's place on his table. When he returned to his seat, he expected to see a message of anger and bitterness. Instead he read:

"... and who knoweth whether thou art come to the kingdom for such a time as this?" (Esther 5:14). DLG.

28: The "Refounding Fathers"

After the political leaders of North America returned from France, with the satisfaction of knowing that their efforts helped to reshape positively the future of the postwar world, they set about positively reshaping the future of North America.

Woodrow Wilson, Hoke Smith, Elbert Thomas, and Will Rogers, called by some humourists (including Rogers himself) the "Refounding Fathers" discussed at length the future of North America on the voyage from Le Havre to New York, and then for a further week in Princeton before each set off by train.

They decided that getting a proposal to the people in late 1920 was essential. November 1920 was one of those rare occasions when the presidential election cycles coincided for the Union (four-year term), the Confederacy (five year term), and Deseret (six-year term). As each of the three republics went to the polls on the same day, so also should the proposal to reunify be put to all the people at once on that day as well.

The decision was that, on Election Day of 1920, this proposal would be put to the public:

- The Union, the Confederacy, Deseret, Texas, and the Protectorates of Oklahoma, New Mexico, and Arizona should all reunite as a single republic – to be called The United States of America - on the 12th of August 1926, the sixty-fifth anniversary of the surrender of Fort Sumter.

- In the event that Confederate officials succeed in re-establishing the rule of law and the re-creation of democratic institutions in Texas before the date of Reunification, the Confederacy shall re-admit Texas as a state at any feasible time before that date.
- While not becoming a state as such, the District of Columbia shall (as of the date of Reunification) be entitled to the same two senators, members of the House of Representatives based in population, and members of the Electoral College based in population as any state.
- If this proposal succeeds, referenda shall be held in the overseas protectorates of Cuba, Puerto Rico, Hawai'i, American Samoa, the American Virgin Islands, Guam, and the Philippines in 1925 to determine which overseas protectorates wish to become independent and which wish to become incorporated into territories becoming states.
- At the time of Reunification, the serving President of the Union shall become President of the reunited USA; while the serving Vice-president of the Confederacy shall become Vice-President.
- The legislative bodies of the Union, the Confederacy, Deseret, Texas, the Protectorates, and each of the states are requested to prepare the necessary constitutional amendments and legislation to make this change possible.

These proposals were put to the public in the November general elections in 1920. They passed with strong support: close to 65% in the Union, close to 70% in Deseret and the Protectorates, close to 76% in the Confederacy, and a massive 87% in Texas.

The election results were wildly diverse. In many cases, the results were good for the Progressives.

- In the Confederacy, the 65-year old Hoke Smith was elected to his fifth five-year term as President, with the 58-year old Oscar Underwood of Alabama elected to his third term as Vice-President.
- The voters of Deseret elected their 37-year old Secretary of State, Elbert Thomas, as President.
- Will Rogers retained his seat as chairman of the Protectorate Council for Oklahoma.

However, in the Union, the Patriotic and the Populist parties decided to run a joint ticket for the 1920 elections. Ohio Senator Warren Harding, from the Pats, ran as President on the joint ticket, with the Pops' perennial presidential candidate, William Jennings Bryan from Nebraska, running as the ticket's vice-presidential candidate. The Progressives ran a ticket led by Ohio Governor James M. Cox, with Assistant Secretary of the Navy Franklin D. Roosevelt (a distant cousin of the former President) as his running-mate. While the Progressives were popular as a party, the combined strength of the Pops and the Pats, particularly in mid-western states, led to the joint ticket winning an unexpected, but narrow, victory over the Progressives.

The Harding-Bryan administration was not a successful one. While Harding appointed some able individuals with high levels of integrity to his cabinet, he also appointed a number of absolute thieves. Harding actively tolerated the corruption of his associates. Many of the scandals which had marked Harding's political reputation only came to public attention after his death in August of 1923.

With Harding's death, and Bryan succeeding to the Presidency, the tone of the administration shifted from cynical corruption to clueless incompetence. The handful of cabinet secretaries (Charles Evans Hughes, Andrew Mellon, and Herbert Hoover) who tried unsuccessfully to combat corruption among their colleagues under Harding, now tried (equally in vain) to establish some sense of discipline and professionalism under Bryan.

By 1924, the country was ready to return the White House to the safe hands of the Progressives, who nominated the Governor of New York, Al Smith, as President, supported by the long-term Wisconsin Senator Robert LaFollette as the Vice-presidential candidate.

Infighting between the Pats and the Pops led to the decision of the two parties to run separate tickets again.

- The Pats ran a ticket of former Massachusetts governor Calvin Coolidge and Secretary of Commerce Herbert Hoover, both of whom were untouched by the Harding-era scandals.
- The Pops renominated Bryan and selected Montana Senator Burton Wheeler as his running-mate.

Given Harding's toleration of rampant corruption and Bryan's toleration of gross incompetence, a strong victory by the Progressive ticket appeared likely. The decision by Bryan (along with a number of Protestant evangelists) to make Al Smith's Catholicism a campaign issue led to a massive public revulsion toward Bryan, and to a Progressive landslide.

From the 1924 election onward to our own day, neither the Pats nor the Pops were ever given a serious hope of winning a presidential election. After Reunification, both minor parties became sources of comedians' one-liners rather than serious contenders to occupy the White House. As far as presidential politics was concerned, the opportunity for the electorate to make a meaningful choice among candidates happened during increasingly robust Progressive Party primaries rather than during general elections.

The 1924 election had a number of other lasting impacts.

After this presidential election, no politician or media figure would ever dare to suggest that a politician's religious affiliation, race, gender, or any other factor would disqualify him or her from serving any office, however high. Al Smith's election not only helped enable the election of the four Catholics who served as President in the years after him, it also helped enabled the election of the three women, the two African-Americans, the two Jews, the two Latter-Day Saints, and the one Native American among Smith's successors.

As well, this election caused a shift in denominational affiliation among many Americans. Many preachers who shared Bryan's denunciation of Smith's Catholicism found themselves preaching to smaller and smaller congregations, both during and after the election. Denominations whose leadership criticised Bryan for making Smith's religious affiliation a campaign issue (particularly Methodists, Episcopalians, and Quakers) grew at the expense of those churches (such as the more conservative variety of Baptists, Lutherans, and Presbyterians) whose leaders excused or even endorsed Bryan's behaviour.

In the years following Reunification, a growing interest in Catholicism developed among many Americans, particularly (but not only) among African-Americans and among Southerners. In every decade since then, a number of high-profile conversions have taken place. Cardinal William ("Billy") Graham was a Presbyterian theological student when he converted to Catholicism. He was involved in the conversion of his close friend, former President Jimmy Carter, soon after he concluded his Presidential term. Another presidential convert was Barry Obama, who converted before becoming President, while serving as Vice-President to Joe Biden. High profile converts within the world of entertainment and the media have included Elvis Presley, Dolly Parton, Aretha Franklin, and Oprah Winfrey.

One interesting factor here was that, unlike many adult converts to Catholicism elsewhere in the English-speaking world, these converts did not gravitate to the ultra-conservative wing of the Church but, instead, embraced a more pragmatic, inclusive, and ecumenical approach to Catholicism, such as practiced by the majority of "cradle Catholics". (Some historians say this was at least partly a result of the example of the noted nineteenth century American convert Bishop William Lincoln, who always pursued an inclusive approach to his faith.)

Anyway, things moved quickly after the 1924 election. Referenda were held in the overseas protectorates. To nobody's surprise, the Philippines voted in favour of independence (which it eventually received in 1936), while Hawai'i, Puerto Rico, Cuba, Guam and the American sections of Samoa and the Virgin Islands opted for a process leading to statehood. The territories of The American Pacific and The American Caribbean were organised, to come into formal existence at the time of Reunification. (Both received statehood in 1959.)

Texas was readmitted as a state of the Confederacy at the beginning of 1925, once a legislature had been elected, and a few honest and competent judges appointed.

In the summer of 1925, Robert LaFollette died, leaving the administration without a Vice-president. His death was followed by the death of William Jennings Bryan a month later.

In November of 1925, the Confederacy had its last scheduled general elections before Reunification. Hoke Smith and Oscar Underwood were re-elected unopposed.

In Washington, Al Smith appointed a cabinet with a largely interim "feel" to it, with a few exceptions. Smith wanted to have space for some appointees from the Confederacy, Deseret, and the Protectorates after Reunification, so a number of cabinet positions were filled by elder statesmen (who were generally also elder*ly* statesmen) who were more than willing to retire at the time of Reunification.

A few appointees who were not seen as temporary included Franklin Roosevelt at Treasury, Gifford Pinchot at Interior, Frances Perkins at Labor (the first woman in an American cabinet), and *Florestan Johnson* at the War Department. (Not only was *Florestan Johnson* the first African-American in an American cabinet, he was also – despite the rantings of Bryan about a "Rome-riddled administration" – the only Catholic in Smith's cabinet.)

At the end of the Great War, *Johnson* retired from the Army as a Brigadier General and returned to the family's stockbroking firm. He was persuaded to return to public life by Smith. By that time, his twin sons were both sophomores and promising sportsmen at Notre Dame and were each expressing their interest in getting into either of the "family businesses. *Faust,* an economics major and a key member of Knute Rockne's offensive line, the "Seven Mules", was also interested in the world of stocks and bonds. *Falstaff,* a history major and a brilliant curve-ball pitcher, wanted to enter the world of military intelligence.

After Reunification in 1926, Smith's Cabinet was enhanced by the presence of former members of the

Confederate, Deseret, and Protectorates administrations. Former Confederates in the cabinet included Oscar Underwood as Vice-President, Hoke Smith as Attorney-General, and the promising Texan representative Sam Rayburn at Commerce. Rayburn and Franklin Roosevelt made a formidable team in the Administration's efforts to prevent the 1929 recession from turning into something far worse.

Both Oscar Underwood and Hoke Smith declared their wish to serve only the remainder of the 1924 term in these roles, with each wanting to retire at the end of the term. Underwood was succeeded as Vice-President for Smith's second term by the Secretary of Agriculture, Will Rogers, from the former Protectorates. Hoke Smith was succeeded as Attorney-General by the bold, Italian-American (albeit with a Jewish mother) reformer, New York Congressman Fiorello LaGuardia.

One of the shining stars of the Smith Administration was the Secretary of State, Elbert Thomas. Thomas, who formerly served Deseret both as Secretary of State and as President, was widely regarded as one of the great US Secretaries of State, in a class with a William Seward or a Ralph Bunche. Thomas served as Secretary of State under four presidents: Al Smith, Will Rogers, Sam Rayburn, and Frances Perkins, before serving as Fiorello LaGuardia's Vice-president. After LaGuardia's death from cancer in 1947, Thomas briefly served as President, making him the first of two Mormons (the other being George Romney, elected in 1968 after serving as Vice-president in the Bunche Administration) to occupy the White House.

Late in 1925, after the relevant constitutional amendments and pieces of enabling legislation had passed each of the national congresses and state legislatures, the formal announcement was made. The Union, the Confederacy (including Texas), Deseret, and the Protectorates were scheduled to formally reunite as the United States of America at 12:00 noon, Eastern Standard Time, on 12th April 1925, the 65th anniversary of the initial breakup of the United States. The formal ceremony of Reunification was to be held at the place where the breakup effectively began, Fort Sumter, in the harbour of Charleston, South Carolina.

29. "A mighty woman with a torch"

Fort Sumter, Charleston Harbour, South Carolina, 12th April 1926.

Colonel Dave Lincoln sat in his dress uniform in an uncomfortable wooden folding chair in one of the first few rows facing the temporary stage of the parade ground in Fort Sumter. He had a few reasons to be assigned a seat so close to the stage in the VIP section. As the grandson of Abe Lincoln, he had some connection to the history of this day. As the head of military intelligence, he had reason to be present to supervise the security arrangements. He was also there as a parent of a participant in the programme.

Dave's teenage daughter *Leah Lazarus Lincoln*, was now reading a poem written by *Dave*'s mother, a poem about another great structure in another great harbour on the coast of this continent, a poem about "a mighty woman with a torch", a torch which "glows world-wide welcome" to all who seek hope, and which declares to the Old World, "Keep, ancient lands, your storied pomp!" *Dave* heard *Leah* finish the poem, reading words which *Dave*'s own mother wrote in 1883 when *Dave* was a baby.

"... Give me your tired, your poor,
Your huddled masses yearning to breathe free,
The wretched refuse of your teeming shore.
Send these, the homeless, tempest-tossed to me,
I lift my lamp beside the golden door!"

Following her family tradition, *Leah Lazarus Lincoln* would spend much of her own life in public service. Her teaching career at Brandeis would be interrupted by two ambassadorial appointments, one in the mid-1950s to the Federation of Israel and Palestine and one in the late 1960s to the Irish Free State. As the US Ambassador in Dublin, she would win a Nobel Peace Prize for her leadership in negotiating a peaceful settlement to a brief civil war between the Irish Free State and a guerilla movement of Presbyterian separatists in the northern region of Ireland.

But back to 1926 and to the Reunification ceremony: after the applause, shared by the author of those words and her granddaughter reading them, it was time for the ceremony itself.

Four anthems were to be played while flags were lowered on smaller, temporary flagpoles set up behind the stage, within the fort's parade ground. After this, there was to be silence, until the bells of Charleston city could be heard ringing the hour of twelve noon. Then the flag of the new, reunited nation was to be raised. After that, there were oaths of office to be taken and speeches to be given.

The first anthem was "The Battle Hymn of the Republic", played as a flag with thirteen stripes and thirty-five stars was lowered. It was followed by Deseret's "Come, Come, ye Saints" and the unofficial anthem of the Protectorates "Home on the Range", as the corresponding flags were lowered. As the Confederacy's flag with its blue saltire and white stars on its red background was lowered, the band played "Dixie". Tears appeared in Hoke Smith's eyes, remembering the time when he heard it in a conference hall in Paris. His soon-to-be colleagues in Al

Smith's cabinet, Elbert Thomas and Will Rogers, each shook his hand warmly as the band played.

Then, with about three minutes to go before noon, it was time for silence. It was a profound silence. For most, it was a prayerful silence, with the image of the "mighty woman with a lamp", glowing "world-wide welcome" directing the content of the prayers. Many, including Al Smith, were on their knees, some with rosaries in their hands. Of the majority who were standing, a few (including *Dave Lincoln*) had put on yarmulkes and prayer shawls. The proverbial pin dropping would have reverberated around the silent parade ground.

Eventually, a distant bell began to ring. It was joined by others, all ringing the hour of twelve noon. The colour guard proceeded to the large flagpole erected on the wall of the fort, to raise a new flag. It was like the first flag which was lowered a few minutes before, with its thirteen stripes. This flag, though, had fifty stars, one each for the thirty-states of the old Union, the eight states of the old Confederacy (including Texas), the three states of the old Protectorates, Deseret (now to be called Utah, following a referendum earlier in the year), the District of Columbia, and the two overseas Territories of the American Caribbean and the American Pacific.

While no official anthem was yet chosen for the reunified nation, the band played an old song describing a battle fought in the War of 1812, a clearly appropriate choice given the site of today's ceremony at Fort Sumter, thought

Dave. Paul Robeson's booming *basso profundo* clearly enunciated each word:

*"O say, does that Star-Spangled Banner yet wave,
o'er the land of the free and the home of the brave."*

Afterwards, as people got off their feet or their knees, as they resumed their seats, as they dried their tears, and as they put their rosaries and yarmulkes back in their pockets, it was time for the politicians and the judges, for the oaths of office and the speeches.

Dave Lincoln didn't remember much of what followed, in all honesty. Dave's thoughts on that Spring afternoon in Charleston Harbour were with his mother who died in New York when he was a little boy, and with his daughter, who made his mother's words sing with urgency. Nevertheless, along with all the other descendants of Abe and Mary Lincoln, *Dave* had a train to catch that evening. In three days' time (along with his father, his uncles, his daughter, and a few cousins), *Dave* had an appointment in a cemetery in Springfield, Illinois, with his late grandparents and with a bottle of French cognac.

"Today was another victory for the '*better angels of our nature*'," thought *Dave*. "*I lift my lamp beside the golden door!*"

Why I wrote this book

Counterfactual histories

Reading counterfactual histories has long been one of my intellectual "guilty pleasures".

Now, let me clarify this.

- On the one hand, I don't mean that my guilty pleasure is the promotion of "alternate facts" as reality in "a post-truth world" as exemplified by some populist politicians and media figures, particularly by those on the extreme right. In contrast, I don't believe that anyone has the right (or the ability) to have their own private "truth" (or "truthiness") or their own personal "facts". The Holocaust actually happened. So did the Irish Potato Famine. People actually landed on the moon. Truth is truth. Facts are facts. History is history. Fiction is fiction. This book is a work of fiction.

- On the other hand, I don't mean that my guilty pleasure is the science fiction-type of counterfactual, in which historical figures or characters from literary classics (or both) share the pages of the book with vampires, zombies, or Martians. I'm sorry, but I just don't "get" that sort of book. I personally believe that counterfactuals (such as this book) need to be a "sub-genre" of historical fiction, not of science fiction and fantasy.

If you were expecting either of these approaches in this book, I'm sorry to disappoint you. (*But thank you in any event for your generous contribution to the Robert J. Faser Annual Vacation and Christmas Shopping Fund.*)

My guilty pleasure is that I enjoy reading books and articles which pose a "what if?" scenario and seek to answer the question of how history may have been changed if one decision had been different, or if the outcome of one event (or a series of events) had been altered.

"What if Hitler had decided not to invade Russia?"

"What if Napoleon had won at Waterloo?"

"What if Catherine of Aragon provided Henry VIII with a male heir?"

(Warning to the reader: If I attempt to write another counterfactual, I'll probably follow the Henry VIII / Catherine of Aragon route.)

The good examples of this style of writing seek to impose a logical cause-and-effect process on the alternative historical narrative they develop. The economic, military, political, social, cultural, scientific, and technological factors correspond closely in the alternate scenario to those which occurred in real life. As well, historical individuals in a good counterfactual are of a similar moral character as they were in reality. Occasions for an improbable *deus ex machina* (including Martians, vampires, and zombies *ex machina*) are rare.

To illustrate this process of cause-and-effect in terms of one chain of counterfactual events in this book:

1. The basis of the scenario of this book is that the American Civil War was avoided.

2. As a result of this scenario, the situation did not develop in which those on both sides who fought and survived did not return home with a host of violent memories which they needed to put out of their minds, with excessive drinking being one popular response to the violent memories.

3. As a result, alcoholism and public drunkenness was far less of a social problem in late-19th century America in this scenario than it was in reality.

4. As a result, temperance movements chose not to focus on promoting total abstinence from alcohol, but on encouraging those who choose to drink to do so intelligently.

5. As a result, the movement to ban the manufacture, importation, and sale of alcoholic beverages in America did not grow in popular support.

6. As a result, Prohibition did not happen.

7. As a result, criminal organisations did not develop an undeservedly high level of popular support in the community as a result of their providing illicit liquor to populations denied access to legal liquor.

8. As a result, the influence of organised crime in politics, business, and popular culture in the United

States today is far lower in this scenario than in reality.

There is a logical cause-and-effect progression in a good counterfactual. However, such works are still *fiction*, and openly so. This book is a work of fiction. Let me repeat this, in case it didn't register. ***This book is a work of fiction.***

Counterfactuals and the American Civil War

One particularly popular area for the writers of counterfactual history deals with the outcome of the American Civil War. How would history have changed either if the South won, or if the war never happened in the first place? (Please note that I began writing this book before either HBO's series *Confederate* or Amazon's series *Black America* were announced, and completed it before either was broadcast. This book should not be seen as a response to either television series. I am in no position to evaluate either, as neither has yet been broadcast. This book explores a different counterfactual result to the sectional conflict than those which were the premises of either series.)

I'm sad to say that many of the counterfactual books exploring this theme of alternate results to the Civil War are of dubious worth. Sometimes they promote a destructive white supremacist viewpoint. Sometimes they express an excessively romantic view of antebellum Southern society, frequently known as "the Cult of the

Lost Cause". These books are, in my opinion, well worth avoiding.

In my opinion, two particularly good counterfactuals about an alternative result for the US Civil War are MacKinlay Kantor's ***If The South Had Won the Civil War*** (1960) and Harvey Ardman's ***ReUnion*** (2014).

Kantor's classic, written in a journalistic style, has the Confederacy winning the war as a result of two dramatic changes of fortune in July 1863: the deaths of both Grant and Sherman during the Vicksburg campaign and the dramatic success of Lee's strategy at Gettysburg, followed by the Confederacy capturing Washington and the secession of most of the border states.

Ardman's more recent novel sets the scene with a scenario similar to this book. The American Civil War did not happen at all. Lincoln chose to avoid war by allowing the South to secede.

There are aspects to the narrative of both books with which I'd differ.

In Kantor's book, the relations between North and South became too normal too quickly, in my opinion. A destructive war took place, if not for four years, at least for two. Nevertheless, Kantor describes the relations between the Union and the Confederacy becoming as cordial as the relations today between, say, Australia and New Zealand almost immediately, without a long period of mistrust akin to the Britain-Ireland relationship prior to the Good Friday Agreement. This, in my opinion, runs counter to human nature. It takes a long time – at least a generation - for people's emotions to really get over a war, even a brief one.

In Ardman's book, almost the polar opposite happened. Even though the War Between the States did not happen, the level of mutual mistrust and contempt between North and South was similar to the level of mistrust and contempt which occurred in reality as a result of the Civil War, Reconstruction, the rise of the Ku Klux Klan, and the development of the Jim Crow system.

As well, the Southern culture depicted in Ardman's book was a culture such as existed in much of the Deep South prior to the late twentieth century: a dysfunctional culture which (in reality) was created by war, Reconstruction, and reaction; a culture of systematised racial discrimination, religious fundamentalism, and a semi-feudal social system. If the War Between the States did not take place, as in Ardman's scenario, a radically different South – with a radically different culture - may have developed compared to the culture of the South which (in our reality) existed for much of the time between Reconstruction and the Civil Rights movement. This is a premise of this book.

My final criticism of Ardman's book is the confusing international scene. Canada is not a single nation. Ontario became part of what remained of the United States. Quebec (presumably including the Maritime Provinces) and Western Canada (or "Canadia") are two separate independent nations. (I personally like the idea of Vancouver being a national capital, however.) The dominant power in North America is a fascist Mexico, closely allied with Imperial Germany (which became the dominant world power following its victory in the Great War).

However, notwithstanding these criticisms, these books by Kantor and Ardman are easily my favourite Civil War counterfactuals.

The scenario of this book

In this book, I seek to explore what could have happened if Abraham Lincoln chose not to pursue a military option when faced with the secession of the Confederate States. "The better angels of our nature," to which Lincoln appealed in his Inaugural Address in 1861, led Lincoln to a decision to surrender Fort Sumter, to reject the prospect of war, and to accept as a "necessary evil" the secession of those states that left the Union. In response, the majority of slave states that had not yet seceded took a "wait and see" attitude toward secession, and remained in the Union. (As Virginia did not secede, West Virginia never became a separate state.) State governments in these states adopted legislation providing for the gradual emancipation of their slaves.

In the Confederacy, a worsening economy led to a military coup in 1864, with the resulting junta also establishing gradual emancipation. In response to the Confederate coup and to gradual emancipation, Texas seceded from the Confederacy and invited the deposed Mexican Emperor Maximillian to serve as its head of state. By the time a fully civilian government was restored in the Confederacy in 1880, slavery was functionally non-existent on the North American continent, with the exception of the Empire of Texas (where it continued until both slavery and the Empire itself were abolished by the Treaty of Versailles following the Great War).

Further west, the Utah Territory capitalised on the precedent set by the secession of the southern states and declared its independence as the Commonwealth of Deseret. Also, the Indian Territory (the present-day state of Oklahoma) and the Territory of New Mexico (the present-day states of New Mexico and Arizona) became the Protectorates, self-governing lands for Native Americans under the shared patronage of the Union, the Confederacy, and (later) Deseret.

This situation continued until the defeat of Texas (along with the other Central Powers) in the Great War.

As a result, there were some real differences in the history which emerged in this counterfactual narrative compared to that of real life.

Relations between the North and the South:

In my scenario, the war known in the Northern United States as the "Civil War" (and known in the Southern US as the "War Between the States") did not happen. Similarly, Reconstruction did not happen. The massive Southern overreaction to Reconstruction did not happen. The "Jim Crow" system of racial discrimination was never established. The Ku Klux Klan was never founded.

The population of the South in the late 19th century, in this scenario, was not one consisting essentially of WASPs and African-American, and not all that much of anyone else, as it was in our reality. Given the economic boom accompanying the end of slavery, the South had plenty of jobs waiting to people to fill them. Thus, the large scale immigration of the late 19th century found its way to the cities of the Confederacy as well as to those of the Union. The ports of Charleston, Savannah, and New Orleans all had their own equivalents to New York's Ellis Island. By the early years of the twentieth century, Southern cities were as ethnically diverse as Northern ones. A South Carolinian didn't have to travel to New York or Pittsburgh to enjoy a pizza, a moussaka, a pierogi, or a bagel.

The cultural perception of Southerners by other Americans was also radically different in my scenario from the one which has predominated for most of the 20th century. Southerners and Northerners were not seen as terribly different to each other. In terms of depicting the culture of the South, while the wry irony seen in the stories of Flannery O'Connor remained, the sense of cultural decay and decadence seen in William Faulkner and Tennessee Williams was not present. In this scenario, Harper Lee's **To Kill a Mockingbird** (in my mind, the "Great American Novel") was set, not in Alabama, but in Texas during the time of transition from the Empire to a restored democracy in the early 1920s.

The popular cultural image of the rural, white, male Southerner in this scenario is not our existing stereotype which varies from a charmingly casual, Burt Reynoldsesque "good old boy" at best, to the monsters of ***Mississippi Burning*** and ***Deliverance*** at worst, with the stereotypical average being an amiable buffoon in the tradition of Jethro Bodine and Gomer Pyle. In this scenario, Tom Hanks still received the 1994 Best Actor Oscar, but for playing the title role in the film ***Olaf Gumpersen***, about a "simple man" from a rural community in northern Minnesota.

Relations between African-Americans and other communities:

Relations between African-Americans and other communities both in the Confederacy and in the Union were simpler and more positive in this scenario than in reality. Slavery was phased out, and it wasn't replaced by "Jim Crow". When African-Americans ceased to be slaves, they became citizens with full legal, political, and economic rights. ... Period. ... Full stop. ... Game, set, and match. ... Thank you, linespeople. Thank you, ball kids. ... The fat lady is singing.

The other thing here was that the end of slavery in this scenario was good for the economy. The grants made to former slaves and the compensation paid to former slaveowners provided a massive injection of cash into the economies both of the Confederacy and of the slave states which remained in the Union. By 1880, hardly any slaves were field hands, and the Confederacy was no longer an economic "basket case".

In this scenario, the handful of people remaining as slaves by 1890 were household servants. *Figaro Johnson*, the last known person to be a slave in either the Union or Confederacy, was a butler in Nashville until he was freed in 1893. In *Johnson's* case, his emancipation was based on the fact that he had one of the most brilliant (if self-taught) financial minds of his era. Over the years, he had made millions for his owner, for his owner's friends and relations, and for himself. He was freed as the result of a hot stock market tip.

By the time of the Great War, the relations between black and white Americans on both sides of the border were essentially normalised. A black and a white person being married to each other was unremarkable, as was a white person working for a black employer. Race did not remain the Great American Obsession (particularly for people of a conservative political or social temperament) in this narrative that it has been in our reality.

In contrast to our reality, African-Americans outside the Confederacy remained almost as rural a community as those living in the Confederacy. For much of the period covered in this narrative, more than half of black Americans, in both North and South, were farmers.

The Great Migration of rural African-Americans to the cities in the early decades of the twentieth century still happened in this scenario. Those who relocated to northern and West Coast cities tended to be those already living within the Union. Those living in the Confederacy were more apt to relocate to southern cities. The Harlem

Renaissance of the 1920s was accompanied by similar flowerings of cultural creativity in New Orleans, Atlanta, Savannah, and Charleston.

The impact of race relations on popular culture was still a creative one. In particular, black and white musicians still encouraged and challenged each other's creativity. However, the whole process was far less clandestine than it was on our reality (at least in its earliest stages). Nevertheless, it happened, and it happened as well and as creatively in this scenario as it did in reality. (As an author, I find I face a moral dilemma here. Just as I would not have wanted to rob the world's culture of the music of Handel, Bach, or Mozart, so also would I not want to deprive the world – even in the fictionalised scenario of a counterfactual - of the music of Scott Joplin or George Gershwin, ... of Duke Ellington or Benny Goodman, ... of Louis Armstrong or Dave Brubeck, ... of Billie Holliday or Patsy Cline, ... of Ray Charles or Elvis Presley, ... of Aretha Franklin or Dolly Parton.)

Deseret and the Latter-Day Saints

In the Commonwealth of Deseret, the home of the Latter-Day Saints (or "Mormons"), other factors enter into this scenario. While we today think of the Mormons in terms of flamboyantly excessive social conservatism, particularly in terms of issues relating to sex and gender, such was not always the case.

Early Mormon history always seemed to constitute a struggle between the social creativity and the optimistic view of human nature exemplified in their founder, Joseph Smith, and the social conservatism of Smith's successor, Brigham Young. In this scenario, with Deseret achieving its independence during the time of Young's leadership, the stage was set for a return to more charismatic, visionary, and optimistic leadership in the tradition of Smith (and provided by Smith's eldest son), after Young's death.

Much of the excessive social conservatism that has marked Mormons in reality during the decades since they abandoned polygamy following 1890 seem to me to have been grounded in the attempt by Latter-Day Saints to become socially accepted in the United States. In so doing, they needed to rid themselves of the popular cultural stereotype of the Mormon male as an oversexed polygamist, adopting an extreme version of the Puritan family as their social ideal in response.

Instead, in an independent Deseret, Mormons were free to be themselves. They abandoned polygamy almost a decade earlier in this scenario than they did in reality. However, they did so for their own reasons, rather than for the purpose of making themselves look respectable in the eyes of Bostonians and Philadelphians.

In this scenario, the Commonwealth of Deseret became a place, not of staid social conservatism, but of pioneering social experimentation, grounded in the strong sense of optimism regarding human nature and co-operative effort toward achieving shared communal goals that, since the days of Joseph Smith, have always marked Latter-Day Saints at their best.

Relations between Native Americans and other communities:

Relations between Native Americans and other communities were far better in this scenario than in reality, for two reasons:

1. The existence of the self-governing Protectorates meant that Native Americans had a large and substantial region where they essentially governed themselves in all areas other than foreign policy. Native Americans who chose to continue living in the area of their tribal lands knew they always had the option of living in the Protectorates.

2. The fact that the Civil War did not happen means that the Union Army was without a large supply of bored officers looking for their next battle or skirmish, thinking "If we can't fight Johnny Reb, the Sioux will do." Without these officers spoiling for a fight, there were far less occasions of armed conflict on the frontier, making the West far less "wild" in this scenario than in reality.

Religion in America

The overwhelming influence of evangelical-fundamentalist styles of Protestant Christianity within the culture of the South, largely a reaction to the post-Civil War social dislocation of many Southerners, did not happen in this scenario. Revivalist forms of conservative Protestant faith were found in the South, as they were in the North, but, in my scenario, people living in the Confederacy were as likely as those living in the Union to be Catholics, Jews, Episcopalians, middle-of-the-road Protestants, atheists, or agnostics. In fact, in this scenario, Southerners today tend to see over-the-top evangelical fervour as "a Yankee thing".

While we're on the subject of religion, although religious identification and practice are even higher than they are in our reality, evangelical Protestant fundamentalism, in both North and South, is a far lesser force in American life in this scenario than in our reality. Conservative evangelicalism never became a major social force in the South. In the North, it lost much of its credibility as a result of the involvement of many prominent evangelical preachers in the campaign against Al Smith's presidential bid in 1924. The separated northern and southern wings (and the separated black and white wings) of many denominational traditions reunited by the time of Reunification in 1926.

In this scenario, then, Roman Catholicism is the largest denomination nationally in our day, followed by Methodists, Episcopalians, and Quakers, with these being the four strongest denominations in both North and South, and among both Blacks and Whites. Lutherans and Latter-Day Saints are regionally significant denominations. Presbyterians and members of the various strands of Judaism (with over 80% of American Jews identifying as Reform) are strong among the urban and suburban middle classes in all regions. Texas has a significant Muslim minority, largely as a result of Turkish soldiers requesting to settle in Texas following their release from prisoner-of-war camps at the end of the Great War.

American politics:

In this scenario, American politics developed a three-party system, as opposed to its present two-party system, in the midst of the nineteenth century. Today, the extreme Right is far less of a potent force in the United States in this scenario than in our reality, particularly given the factors that, during the mid-twentieth century, the far Right had no Cold War to fight and no Civil Rights movement to oppose (and, therefore, no real *raison d'etre* during the period in which – in reality - it sadly grew dramatically as a movement). Many iconic far-right-wing figures of the period from the mid-twentieth century to the present in our reality had (in this scenario) quiet, obscure, and reasonably contented careers outside politics as real estate agents, insurance salesmen, car dealers, divorce lawyers, cosmetic surgeons, and restauranteurs. As a result, the US is a far happier place today in this scenario, even if its politics is somewhat more boring, than it is in our reality. *(Given the alternative, I can do boring. RJF.)*

The wider world:

Unlike Ardman's complex alternate world scene, there are few differences between reality and this scenario (at least until the end of the Great War) in terms of events in the world outside the borders of today's Continental United States. (After the end of the Great War, all bets are off.)

1. Canadian history is unchanged.

2. The only difference in terms of Mexican history is that the Emperor Maxmillian fled to Texas rather than remaining in Mexico and facing a firing squad.

3. Seward was unsuccessful in his attempts to persuade the Senate to buy Alaska from Russia.

4. In the Spanish-American War, the Union and Confederacy were allied in fighting Spain.

5. In the Great War, Texas sided with the Central Powers. At the same time, the Union, the Confederacy, Deseret, and the Protectorates supported the Allies from the outbreak of the War in 1914.

The lives and careers of individuals:

As a result of the War Between the States not taking place, there are changes in the life-span, life circumstances, and careers of many individuals. (Although, in any good counterfactual, historical individuals display a similar character in the world of the counterfactual to the one they displayed in reality.)

First and foremost, the many people who died as a result of the war, and who were largely unknown, unheralded, and unsung, had longer lives. Those who were wounded and maimed had healthier lives. Those, both civilians and in uniform, who were traumatised by the conflict lived far less troubled lives.

And then, for those individuals who were known to history:

- In this scenario, **Abraham Lincoln** was not assassinated in 1865, but travelled to Britain, Ireland, Europe, the Middle East, India and Australia after concluding his presidential term. During his time abroad, he lived, first in Britain, and then in the Australian state of Tasmania, working as a journalist and lecturer, before returning to America after eleven years abroad.

- **John Wilkes Booth** still fired a shot in anger in a theatre at a political leader on Good Friday of 1865, but the city wasn't Washington, the leader wasn't Lincoln, Booth missed, and the politician managed to "steal the show" from Booth. Booth spent the rest of his life in a psychiatric hospital.

- **Stephen A. Douglas** wasn't in Chicago to contract typhoid in June of 1861, so he lived to be an unsuccessful presidential candidate once again in 1864.

- After his term as Vice-President, **Hannibal Hamlin** served as Lincoln's successor in the White House.

- Because his health wasn't weakened by spending four years in his late fifties living under battlefield conditions, **Robert E. Lee** did not die of a stroke in

1870, but served as Hamlin's Vice-President, completed a term as President himself. and survived into his eighties, as did Lincoln.

- Even if he was unsuccessful in persuading the Senate to consent to purchase Alaska from Russia, **William H. Seward** was one of the great Secretaries of State in US history, serving in both the Lincoln and Hamlin administrations.

- After the Confederate coup in 1864, a junta led by Generals **P.G.T. Beauregard** and **James Longstreet**, along with the civilian politician-diplomat **Judah P. Benjamin**, avoided the South's financial collapse, enabled the end of slavery, and laid a solid foundation for the establishment of a renewed democracy in 1880.

- Because large numbers of soldiers were not quartered in Washington, causing massive problems of poor sanitation leading to widespread disease (as happened in our reality), Lincoln's middle son **William** survived to adulthood. So did his younger brother **Tad**. Both younger Lincoln boys spent some of their young adult years in England, where they were friends of royalty and other notable individuals, before returning to distinguished careers in different fields in America.

- Lincoln's eldest son **Robert Todd Lincoln** became the second presidential son to occupy the White House himself, serving from 1893 to 1897.

- Abe Lincoln's wife, **Mary Todd Lincoln**, enjoyed good physical and mental health until her death from a stroke in 1882.

- **Thomas Jackson** and **J.E.B. Stuart** were not killed in a war which never happened (and Jackson earned the nickname "Stonewall", not in a battle in Virginia which never happened but in a skirmish with Texan bandits near a town in what is now Oklahoma). They spent their careers as professional officers in a peacetime army (along with colleagues such as **Ulysses S. Grant** and **William Tecumseh Sherman**), alternating between serving in forts along the border between the Protectorates and Texas and desk jobs in Washington.

- **Thomas Francis Meagher** did not raise an Irish-American regiment and serve as a Union general in a war which didn't happen. Neither was he later appointed as Governor of the Montana Territory, drowning in mysterious circumstances. Instead the former Irish rebel served as a United States diplomat in Salt Lake City during the Lincoln administration and in Montgomery in the Hamlin administration. He was Seward's successor as Secretary of State, and retired from public life to be a noted boulevardier, raconteur, and wit in New York.

- One officer who found North American military life in the 1860s overly boring was **George Armstrong Custer**, who resigned his commission as soon as he was legally able to do so. He travelled to France to enlist in the one military organisation in the world most suited to a man of Custer's temperament: the French Foreign Legion. After receiving a wound (possibly self-inflicted, according to some sources) in a skirmish in North Africa, Custer automatically received French citizenship and was eligible for an officer's commission in the Legion. Following his retirement from the Legion, Colonel Custer was a colourful figure in the streets, cafés, and salons of 1890s Paris. He was a friend of **Captain Alfred Dreyfus** and (to his credit) was an early and robust public defender of Dreyfus.

Into the Twentieth Century:

If we bring this scenario forward into the twentieth century, we'll find a few more changes. Rather than the United States waiting until 1917 to enter the Great War, in this scenario, we find that the Union, the Confederacy, Deseret, and the Protectorates were all part of the Allies from 1914. Meanwhile Texas joined Germany, Austria, and Turkey in the Central Powers.

After the Treaty of Versailles, history for both the North American continent and for the wider world is radically different in this scenario than in reality:

- Prohibition did not happen, as mentioned earlier.
- The Wall Street Crash of 1929 resulted in a serious (but manageable) national recession lasting three

years or so, rather than in a decade-long, worldwide Great Depression.

- The Nazis never came to power in Germany.

- Because the Nazis never came to power, there was no Holocaust.

- Stalin was overthrown in Russia following the Famine of 1932-33. Tsar Alexei returned from exile in Alaska (where he was visiting at the time of the Revolution, along with his sister Anastasia) to re-establish the Romanoff Dynasty as a limited, constitutional monarchy on the British model.

- There was no European conflict from 1939 to 1945, but there was a war in the Pacific and in Asia in the early 1940s between Japan, on one hand, and the English-speaking nations, on the other. (In this scenario, Humphrey Bogart played a cynical expat American nightclub owner finding his personal life caught up with wartime politics in the classic film ***Noumea***.)

- There was no Cold War.

- Given that former slaves in both the Union and the Confederacy had achieved full citizenship rights by the end of the nineteenth century (and economic and social equality by the end of the Great War), there was no need for a Civil Rights movement in the United States.

- South Africa had a four decades-long civil war between its multiracial government and an Afrikaans-speaking rebel state. During this lengthy conflict, the USA, the UK, and a number of Commonwealth countries (including Canada, Australia, New Zealand, the Irish Free State, and the Federation of Israel and Palestine) provided military assistance to the government. (This conflict provided the setting for the television series *M*A*S*H* and much of the context for the film ***Olaf Gumpersen***.)

- And ... on April 11, 1926, on the 65th anniversary of Lincoln's order to surrender Fort Sumter, the Union, the Confederacy, Deseret, the Protectorates, and Texas all came together to re-form the United States of America.

In this scenario, many things in the twentieth century were different than they were in reality. Many people lived longer lives than they did in our reality. Many followed far different career paths, both for the well-known, and those who were unknown, unheralded, and unsung.

To give a few examples (some of whom are mentioned elsewhere in this narrative, while others are not):

- **Sir Elie Wiesel** was the Principal Conductor of the London Symphony Orchestra until his death last year.

- **Dietrich Bonhoeffer** served as Professor of Theology at Hamburg before becoming the Lutheran bishop of Berlin, with guest lectureships at Princeton, Edinburgh, and Melbourne between his retirement and his death in 1991.

- **David Irving** is the manager of a striptease club in London featuring female or male dancers on different nights. On Wednesday evenings, when his club features "annoyingly fit mature-age male dancers" for the entertainment of "discerning ladies of a certain age", his main acts are an Australian named **Tony Abbott** (billed as "Testosterony Tony"), a Russian named **Vladimir Putin** ("Mad, Bad Vlad"), and a retired New York policeman, **Rudolph Giuliani** ("Rudy the Nudie").

- After Italy's unsuccessful invasion of Ethiopia led to massive rioting, **Benito Mussolini** fled to Japan, where he died in exile. Other exiles living in Japan prior to and during the Pacific War included **General Francisco Franco** (following an unsuccessful coup attempt in Spain), the British politician **Sir Oswald Mosley**, the Irish politician **Eoin O'Duffy,** and a collection of quarrelling German factional leaders. There were a number of firebrand clerics as well, including three Roman Catholic priests, **Marcel Lefebvre** from France, **Josemaria Escriva** from Spain, and **Charles Coughlin** from the United States, along with a number of politicised Protestant evangelists from North America and the deposed Grand Mufti of Jerusalem **Mohammed Amin al-Husseini**, who horrified the British rulers of his region (as well as the majority of Arabs, both Muslim and Christian) by seeking to import European-style antisemitism to the Middle East. Prior to the war, western diplomats and journalists in Tokyo referred to these far-right western expatriates as the "International White Trash" (or IWTs, for short). Following Japan's defeat in the Pacific War, many of the IWTs found their way to Pretoria, where the leaders of the rebellious Boer Free State welcomed their presence as philosophical support.

- **Count Mikhail Gorbachev** recently retired as Russia's foreign minister. Along with the late **Pope John Paul II** (now known as St. John Paul the Peacemaker), he received the Nobel Peace Prize (as well as his title of nobility from the Tsar) in 1991 for negotiating an end to the four-decades-long South African Civil War. (The South African Prime Minister, **Nelson Mandela**, and the President of the then Boer Free State (now part of South Africa again), **F.W. DeKlerk**, received Nobel Peace Prizes - and knighthoods from the Queen – the following year for their role in achieving peace.) Count Gorbachev is still an impressive figure in his dress uniform at such recent international events as the funeral of Sir Nelson Mandela and the canonisation of St. John Paul II and St. John XXIII.

- **Lech Walesa** is an electrical contractor in Gdansk and an active Rotarian.

- Rather than being killed somewhere over the English Channel, **Glenn Miller** lived into his early nineties, and conducted his famous big band well into his mid-eighties. In his later years, he was known for his creative collaboration in albums, concerts, and TV specials with such artists as the Beach Boys, the Four Seasons, Diana Ross, Sir Paul McCartney, Willie Nelson, Leonard Cohen, Tammy Wynette, Stevie Wonder, k.d. lang, and Luciano Pavarotti.

- Until his recent death, **Fidel Castro** was a US Senator from the state of the American Caribbean, and a three-time presidential candidate for the Populist Party. The American Caribbean (Cuba, Puerto Rico, and the US Virgin Islands) and the American Pacific (Hawaii, American Samoa, and Guam) became states of the United States in 1959, bringing the number of states in the US to 49. Castro had served in the Senate since the American Caribbean achieved statehood.

- The social pages of today's edition of the *New York Times* in this scenario includes a reference to a surprise party celebrating the 45th wedding anniversary of the veteran *Times* baseball correspondent (and former catcher for the Pittsburgh Pirates and New York Mets) **Martin Luther King, Jr.** (known as "Doc" during his playing days in the '50s and '60s because he was a member of a then very small number of college graduates who were players in Major League Baseball) and the popular mystery writer **Anne Frank** (creator of the psychiatrist-sleuth Dr. Maureen O'Leary), with both of the couple being described by friends as "incredibly fit and alert at 88". The party, at New York's famous Algonquin Hotel, was hosted by their children, *Congressman Maurice Frank-King* of South Carolina and *Rabbi Juliet Frank-King* of Temple Beth Am in Bayonne, New Jersey. A major part of the surprise for the couple was the presence of each of the living children from the couple's first marriages.

- Speaking of baseball, in this scenario, **Jackie Robinson** was not the first African-American to play major league baseball. Baseball at its highest professional levels was racially integrated since the 1880s. He was still a star player for the Brooklyn Dodgers, however.

- *"The Grumpy Breakfast"*, featuring **Don Imus** and **Bill Cosby**, has been a popular, if controversial, daily breakfast program on national cable TV for the past fifteen years. The program features "caustic commentary on current affairs" (a quote from the program's advertising), high levels of sexual innuendo, frequent fart jokes, and a constant stream of insults by the hosts toward each other, toward **Anthony Weiner** (a former TV game show host who now hosts a similarly crude late night talk show on the same cable network), and toward their guests, particularly their former regular weekly "London correspondent" (until his recent imprisonment), the disgraced British television personality **Rolf Harris**.

- **His Eminence, Cardinal William F. ("Billy") Graham** retired as the Roman Catholic Archbishop of Atlanta in 1993 and recently celebrated his 98th birthday. He converted to Catholicism as a young Presbyterian theological student and became a priest soon after. He became Bishop of Charlotte in 1971 and was a strong advocate of the reforms of the Second Vatican Council and an enthusiastic ecumenist. He was appointed as Archbishop of Atlanta in 1977, and was made a Cardinal by Pope John Paul I in his first consistory. During his time in Atlanta, he received his close friend, former President **Jimmy Carter**, into membership in the Catholic Church. Cardinal Graham was an active member of the conclave that elected Pope John Paul II in 1984 (in which he was considered *papabile* himself), but was too old to be eligible to participate the conclave that elected his good friend Pope Francis in 2005.

- **Donald J. Trump** is a cosmetic surgeon in Las Vegas.

- **Osama Bin Laden** is a soccer coach at a high school in Riyadh.

- **Binyamin Netanyahu** is a dentist in Tel Aviv.

- **Robert Mugabe** owns a Ford dealership in Harare.

- **Kim Jong-Un** manages a McDonald's in Pyongyang.

- **Rodrigo Duterte** is a bouncer at a brothel in Manila.

- **Barack H. ("Barry") Obama** concluded his term as President in January 2017. Before becoming President, he served as a member of the House of Representatives from the state of American Pacific, as Attorney-General in the **Gore** and **Lieberman** administrations, and as Vice-President in the **Biden** administration. He converted to Roman Catholicism while serving as Vice-President. At the end of Barry's term as President, his wife **Michelle** was elected a Senator from the District of Columbia. Barry Obama was succeeded in the Oval Office by the current president, **Caroline Kennedy**, the daughter of one long-serving senator and the niece of two others, who previously served as Secretary of Education in the Biden administration and as Vice-President in the Obama administration.

- **Corporal Adolf Hitler** died of Spanish influenza in a prisoner-of-war camp outside Blairsville, Pennsylvania, in 1918, waiting to be repatriated to Germany after the surrender of his unit at the end of the Texas campaign. Other than to a small number of specialist art historians, to whom he was a minor landscape painter of the early twentieth century, Hitler is unknown to history.

- In 1990, the documentary filmmaker **Ken Burns** released a popular, and critically acclaimed, television series on PBS presenting a chilling counterfactual scenario of what could have happened if Abraham Lincoln was unable to prevent a destructive civil war in North America in 1861.

A personal comment

I began writing this book in early 2017, as a person who
- is US-born,
- who has lived and worked in Australia for most of my adult life,
- who has been a frequent visitor over the years to the land of my birth, and
- who is in regular and frequent contact (via social media) with family members and friends in the United States.

I write with painful awareness of the extent to which the relations between Americans of different racial communities, and between Americans living in different regions of the nation, have continued to provide tragically well-defined fault-lines in American society, culture, and politics, even over a century-and-a-half since the end of the Civil War.

In particular, the fact that race has remained the Great American Obsession (particularly for people of a conservative political and social temperament) has been both a source of great confusion for those living outside the United States and seeking to understand the US, and an occasion of profound heartbreak for those (whether Black, White, or otherwise) living in the United States.

This book is offered in the hope and with the prayer that the description of an alternate history of the relations between the races and the regions may help to heal and to normalise the relations between Black and White, and between North and South, in the United States.

>Robert J. Faser.
>Hobart, Tasmania, Australia
>3rd October 2017

About the Author

Bob Faser grew up in Bayonne, New Jersey, but has spent his adult life in Australia, for the most part in the state of Tasmania.

Bob studied at Lafayette College, Princeton Theological Seminary, the Irish School of Ecumenics, the University of Tasmania, and the Melbourne College of Divinity, where he completed his Doctor of Ministry Studies degree on Christmas in popular culture.

Bob is a retired (recycled?) minister in the Uniting Church in Australia (Congregational, Methodist, and Presbyterian) and has served as a parish minister, an ecumenical staffer, and a hospital chaplain.

Bob is an active Rotarian and an enthusiastic amateur Santa Claus.

Bob's blog *"A Funny Thing Happened on the Way ..."* can be found at http://revdocbob.blogspot.com.au.

This is his first work of fiction.

Made in the USA
Monee, IL
07 September 2020